MATTHEW MAGUIRE: THREE PLAYS

The Tower, Luscious Music, The Desert

NoPassport Press
Dreaming the Americas Series

Matthew Maguire: Three Plays
Copyright 2009 by Matthew Maguire.
"Reaching for Heaven Even as We Burn:
Encountering the Work of Matthew Maguire"
copyright 2008 by Naomi Wallace.

NoPassport Press
Dreaming the Americas Series
First edition 2009 by NoPassport Press
PO Box 1786, South Gate, CA 90280 USA;
NoPassportPress@aol.com, ISBN: 978-0-578-00856-1; $20.00

MATTHEW MAGUIRE: THREE PLAYS

The Tower, Luscious Music, The Desert

CONTENTS

Reaching for Heaven Even as We Burn: Encountering the Work of Matthew Maguire

It is rare to find drama that can challenge, trouble, and revision mainstream American theatre; Matthew Maguire's work does exactly that. The three plays in this new collection, *The Tower*, *Luscious Music*, and *The Desert*, demonstrate a unique theatrical vision in contemporary American theatre. The plays treat, both structurally and thematically, issues of loss, damage, dislocation, and the urgent, perhaps inherent human and social need, to reconstruct and reconnect. With a theatrical eye and ear that fuses the mundane with the metaphysical, Maguire's theatre disassociates us from what we think we know and what we expect to allow for a reimagining of both space and language.

The Tower is a contemporary retelling of the story of the Tower of Babel. While Ruth dreams of secretly rebuilding the tower, she fights for her life on an operating table. The urgency of the play is its characters' need to transcend the earth as prison, both an individual prison, and a social one, and wrestle with God, or the idea of him. As Steven Leigh Morris aptly says in *American Theatre* magazine (Dec. 2004), the play is "part vaudeville, and part religious mass."

But the play is also inherently political. While Ruth wrestles with her own demons, flashes of Gaza, Belfast, Peru, and Kabul continually rupture both her hallucinations and her more contained and isolated life with her husband Jacob. It is in this play where the metaphysical and mundane collide most clearly. And when they do, the play reveals a razor sharp wit and dark sense of humor: Ruth has become obsessed with bitumen, a kind of tar used in the ancient world instead of mortar. This element then seeps into her breakfast, the biblical world and the contemporary colliding. Ruth: "Do you want bitumen for your toast?" and later, "My mouth is a kiln." Maguire never allows Ruth to separate her own struggles from the conflict in the larger world, where war, torture, and famine are intricately linked not only to our future possibilities, but to our individual possibility for transcendence. In the end, while Ruth does not attain paradise, she retains a memory of heaven. This allows her to endure and survive, both the operation and an almost destructive and violent yearning for peace.

The Desert is a play about surviving the loss of broken illusions, and the havoc and damage that illusions wreak on love. In this case, the love is between two sisters, the daughters of diplomats, orphaned at twelve and ten, and now working as croupiers in Vegas. Throughout the play, Marian and Katrine move in and out of fantasy and illusions constructed out of memory. But beyond this, the play is also about the drama of fusion, and an exploration of the forces that cause two people to merge to such an extent that separation can be fatal. Again, as with *The Tower*, language reaches a pressure point where it is broken from its patterned and predictable use, and acquires both new meaning and new power:

MARIAN: You know what I'll do if you get violent.
KATRINE: All right, I'll take you for a waltz through the maze of our garden—remember?
MARIAN: I'm the one who remembers.
KATRINE: The juniper sap used to stick to my fingers and harden like the amber that entombs prehistoric insects. (pause) That memory makes me want to peel the black right off you.

The language here moves from a naturalistic form, to a more formal, poetic utterance. And yet Maguire never allows this movement to seem contrived or sentimental. His is a muscular, graceful poetry and it continually pushes the audience into hearing it anew, and following it to the fresh and strange linguistic and emotional places that it leads.

In one powerful monologue, Marian remembers her reaction to a string quartet she heard as a child, in the company of her family. It is as though the stuffing has been knocked out of her and she sits in that silent moment, before the applause begins, willing this stillness, burned into her by the beauty of the music, to last. But it doesn't last, and finally she herself cannot stop clapping until her father has to clamp her hands shut. The adult Marian asks her sister: "Why couldn't I stop clapping?" and her sister Katrine answers, "What do I do with this grief?" (referring to her abandonment by her husband, an Iraq war veteran). Here is a moment that Maguire controls beautifully, through both language and dramatic structure. The stillness of which Marian speaks once allowed for a suspension of time, and the language she uses to recapture this moment also creates a dramatic stillness in which the play seems to float. Katrine's loss is not the opposite of the rapture Marian once experienced, it is its sister, fused as the two women are, inseparable until they find the moment of their difference.

The most seemingly naturalistic of the three dramas is *Luscious Music*. It is also about two sisters, Clea and Sony Salcedo. Clea and her sister Sony came from Cuba in 1980 in the Mariel boat lift. They lost their family during the crossing in a storm and the tragedy has scarred them both. The play treats the themes of dislocation, but its real theme is about being lost in America. Lost in the American dream. And lost within ourselves, and our inability to accept forgiveness. In this way

Luscious Music and *The Desert* are linked by their pairs of sisters; Marian and Katrine flow from Clea and Sony, forced to grapple with the same crisis for another year.

Again, Maguire links social tragedy to our very personal damage and desires. Maguire's work is never in a vacuum and this is what lends it its scope and depth. And while *Luscious Music* is realistic, the history of Clea and Sony's loss is told in pieces, and we are left only a glimpse of their tragedy, which for its fragmentation is all the more sharp and haunting. A lesser writer might move through these stories towards a vision of healing and reconstruction of personal and social histories. But Maguire has a more challenging proposal for us: how do with live with what is broken and can never be made whole? How do we live and love when so much is missing? Far more than a condition, damage is a process and Maguire tracks this process most closely through Clea's husband, Frank, whose inability to forgive himself for the repeated failures in his life lead him to break down. What is striking about this study of loss and damage is how the play highlights the ever widening reverberations of self-destruction, how our losses are never self-contained and that their potency and poison are often thrown outward onto others. Clea and Sony's parental loss, Frank's loss of self to drugs and hopelessness, Harry's (Sony's lover) lack of a beginning (having been abandoned in a car as a child) all resonate and rebound between them. What Maguire so deftly explores is the ricochet effect of these losses, the collateral damage we wreak upon one another, especially those we love the most.

What links these three plays is their urgency, the breadth of their vision, their language that is always restless even when its metaphors and images are clear and precise. Contemporary theatre is blessed with such a freshly creative mind as Maguire has applied here to our stage. Having come through these stories, one realizes anew that the happenings of this world are deeply, even if often invisibly, inter-connected, that social history cannot be separated from our most intimate relationships, that reaching for heaven, even as we burn, is a worthwhile endeavor. Because as Ruth does, we can retain a memory of heaven, and let it loose on earth.

Naomi Wallace

THE TOWER

The Tower: a Brief History

The Tower was first conceived as an opera with
music by Glenn Branca, and then it took a turn.
Realizing that the medium was new for us, Glenn
and I planned the process as a series of
productions that would act as studies for the
larger work. Robert Stearns at the Walker Art
Center commissioned the first phase, a stage play
with incidental music, co-produced by the Illusion
Theatre in Minneapolis, Michael Robins and
Bonnie Morris, Producing Directors. When John
Killacky began his tenure at the Walker, he
enabled the project to continue. The first
workshops of the play were held at the Illusion
Theatre in October of 1987 and subsequently at
John Kazanjian and Mary Ewald's New City
Theatre in Seattle in January of 1988. It received
its premiere at the Illusion Theater in March, 1989.
The second step was a chamber version that
Creation Production Company produced as a
work-in-progress with Home for Contemporary
Theatre and Art, Randy Rollison, Artistic Director,
in May, 1989. Then we did a site-specific variation
entitled *Babel On Babylon* at Belvedere Castle in
Central Park. This was commissioned by Anne
Hamburger and co-produced with En Garde Arts.
Subsequently, the Meet the Composer/Readers'
Digest Commissioning Program awarded Glenn
and I commissions to begin work on the score and
libretto. With the assistance of a McKnight

Fellowship, the Playwrights Center, and the Minnesota Opera's New Music Theatre Ensemble, I spent two months in Minneapolis working on rewriting the play as libretto. Working with singers was enlightening, as was a subsequent workshop at New Dramatists aided by the direction of Roger Ames. Glenn completed the full score. The next 'variation on the theme' was a solo, *Babel Stories*, which I performed in February 1990. The production of the solo was presented by Primary Stages, Casey Childs, Artistic Director, in association with Creation Production Company. In ensuing years there were several productions, but the Los Angeles theatre company, The Son of Semele Ensemble, Matthew McCray, Artistic Director, produced the one with real impact in 2004. The reason for my extensive acknowledgments is that the current text is the cumulative result of these multiple productions.

The Tower premiered at the Illusion Theater in Minneapolis, March 1, 1989. Michael Robins and Bonnie Morris, Producing Directors. The production was a co-production of the Walker Art Center, the Illusion Theater, and Creation Production Company, directed by the author. The artists involved were:

Ruth	Mary McDevitt
Jacob	Jefferson Slinkard
Dr. Rafel	Alfred Harrison
Dr. Amek	Megan Grundy
Dr. Zabi	Marysue Moses
Music	Glenn Branca
Choreography	Susan Mosakowski
Set Design	Dean Holzman
Light Design	Jeff Bartlett
Costume Design	Katherine Maurer
Dramaturg	Barry Holtz

The next version of *The Tower* was presented at Home for Contemporary Theatre and Art in New York City in May 1989. The artists involved were:

Ruth	Shellye Broughton
Jacob	Anthony Lee
Dr. Rafel	Michael Ryan
Dr. Amek	Isabel Sáez
Dr. Zabi	Kazuki Takase
Set Design	Joe Fyfe
Light Design	Pat Dignan

En Garde Arts commissioned a site-specific version for Belvedere Castle in Central Park. The cast was comprised of a large chorus and two principals: Tessie Hogan and Kevin Davis.

CHARACTERS

RUTH, fighting for her life on the operating table

JACOB, her husband

DR. RAFEL, male, the brilliant but autocratic chief surgeon

DR. AMEK, female, surgeon, an advocate of patients' rights

DR. ZABI, male or female, surgeon, a cautious careerist

A small chorus that plays nurses, prisoners, a tribe of Bedouins, Babylonian masons and a squadron of angels

TIME

From the beginning to the end of a delicate and dangerous surgery.

PLACE

There are three settings that must flow one into another:

- An operating room. The walls glow with the constellations of a winter sky at midnight. The medical machinery appears oversized and ominous.
- RUTH and JACOB's living room in flashback: where unfold the events that lead to her operation.
- A nightmarish zone of prison cells in global crisis spots.

PROLOGUE

THE SOUNDS OF THE OPERATING ROOM ARE HEARD AS THE SURGEONS PREPARE FOR A DANGEROUS EMERGENCY OPERATION ON RUTH'S MOUTH. THE SURGEONS AND NURSES DANCE STIFFLY, ODDLY, AND REPETITIVELY THROUGH THEIR PREPARATIONS.

SCENE 1

ONE LANGUAGE AND FEW WORDS

The Operating Theatre

THE OPERATION IS ABOUT TO BEGIN. AN ARGUMENT HAS ERUPTED OVER JACOB'S SECOND THOUGHTS ABOUT RUTH'S SURGERY.

JACOB: Listen to me! This is not—

DR. RAFEL: Without this operation your wife won't make it.

JACOB: Listen to me! Surgery's not going—

DR. RAFEL: I'm the doctor here, not—

JACOB: You don't understand. You have to—

DR. RAFEL: No, you don't understand, your wife could die.

DR. AMEK: Hear him out.

DR. RAFEL: Get him out of here!

JACOB: I'm staying.

DR. RAFEL: No!

JACOB: You agreed.

DR. RAFEL: No!

DR. AMEK: Dr. Rafel—

DR. RAFEL: The rules strictly forbid—

DR. AMEK: We've seen loved ones bring a patient through.

DR. RAFEL: NO! I'm the chief surgeon!

JACOB: Maybe surgery's not the answer.

DR. RAFEL: And why not?

JACOB: The nightmares.

DR. AMEK: Nightmares?

JACOB: Yes, of prison cells, every—

DR. RAFEL: Psycho-babble.

JACOB: They're the cause—

DR. RAFEL: It's a surgical problem. And she'll die
if we don't start.

JACOB: I'll allow it only if I stay.

DR. ZABI: He's right, Doctor, you've got to have
his consent.

DR. RAFEL: He already signed.

JACOB: I'll hit you with malpractice.

A LONG PAUSE WHILE RAFEL CONSIDERS,
THEN IMPERIOUSLY NODS HIS CONSENT.

DR. RAFEL: Begin.

DR. AMEK: Prep.

DR. ZABI: Starting prep.

RUTH: Jacob?

JACOB: I understand.

DR. ZABI: Pressure?

DR. AMEK: One ten over seventy.

THE OPERATING LIGHTS PULSE.

RUTH: Jacob…

JACOB: Shhhhhhhhh …

RUTH: My mouth …

JACOB: I know … shhhhhhhh … don't talk.

RUTH: … so scared …

JACOB: Shhhhh … still …

PAUSE.

JACOB: Breathe deep, breathe deep, that's it ...

*THE SOUNDS OF HISSING GAS AND DEEP
BREATHING COMBINE AND RISE IN VOLUME.
LIGHTS FADE EXCEPT FOR THE BLUE OF THE
OPERATING TABLE'S GLASS TOP WITH ITS
NEON OUTLINE OF RUTH. WE GLIMPSE A
DESERT LANDSCAPE OF SHIFTING SANDS
AND SWIRLING SKIES AS THE STAGE
CHANGES TO A NIGHTMARE VERSION OF
RUTH AND JACOB'S BEDROOM AS A PRISON
CELL.*

The Prison

*RUTH AND JACOB ARE SLEEPING. RUTH IS
HAVING A NIGHTMARE. PRISONERS IN
BLACK-STRIPED UNIFORMS ADVANCE
RELENTLESSLY UPON HER, HOLDING OUT A
UNIFORM THEY PRESS UPON HER. EACH OF
THEM SINGS IN A DIFFERENT LANGUAGE.
FLASHES OF HEADLINES FROM CRISIS POINTS
AROUND THE WORLD FILL THE AIR AURALLY
AND VISUALLY.*

*RUTH WAKES UP SCREAMING. THE
PRISONERS VANISH.*

JACOB: Ruth, Ruth, Ruth! It's all right, it's only a
dream.

RUTH: It's the same one, over and over.

JACOB: It's all right, it's all right.

RUTH: All I can see is a prison cell.

The House

A SIMPLE PAINTED DROP CAN INDICATE THE HOUSE, PERHAPS A DOLLHOUSE- LIKE CUTAWAY OF ALL THE ROOMS. RUTH AND JACOB READ THE SUNDAY PAPER.

RUTH: Jacob ...

JACOB: Hmmmm ...

RUTH: Did you read this story?

JACOB: Hmm?

RUTH: This story.

JACOB: What's it say?

RUTH: They found the original site of the Tower of Babel.

JACOB: My middle name.

RUTH: These people almost made it to paradise. It's giving me the shivers.

JACOB: Ruth, it's Sunday. Can you rest your awesome digging for one day?

RUTH: This scientist says they felt an unnatural heat rising from the earth—

JACOB: You wanna feel some unnatural heat— come 'ere ...

RUTH: She says the ruins are still seething with heat and ready to erupt to heaven all over again ...

JACOB: That's what I'm saying, now come onnnnnn ....

RUTH: Listen, here's the original story, "Now the whole earth had one language—

JACOB CHASES HER, LAUGHING, AROUND THE HOUSE. THE LAUGHTER BECOMES ORGASMICALLY COLORATURA.

The Bedouin Dance

TWO BEDOUINS WITH LONG FLOWING AZURE VEILS DANCE AN ANCIENT TRIBAL DANCE.

SCENE 2

THE SOUND OF A DISTANT TRAIN

The House

Part 1
Afterglow (Bliss and Babelonia)

RUTH: "And they said to one another, "Come, let us make bricks, and burn them thoroughly.' And they had brick for stone, and bitumen for mortar" ... Bitumen? What's bitumen?

JACOB: It's a lost word, Ruth.

RUTH: Words can't get lost.

JACOB: Old 'woids' never die, they just mutate.

RUTH: (shrieks) Aiiiiiiiiiiii ... Here it is! A footnote! "Bitumen" —it's tar, or asphalt, earthy pitchy stuff like in bituminous coal—what they had for mortar.

JACOB: (gasping) Ohhh ... "bitumen," of course, why didn't you say so! (pause) Ruth ... I feel sort of earthy and pitchy after that big excitement.

RUTH: Oh you poor dear, come here ...

Part 2
A Week Later (The Long Hand of the Lord)

RUTH: Oh no! Jacob! I'm losing it again. There goes the mouth. Oh my Gaw...ddd.

JACOB MOLDS HER MOUTH, COACHING HER THROUGH HER WORDS.

JACOB: That's it. That's it ...

JACOB and RUTH:
OH...MAH...YEE...GAH...DUH!

SHE SNAPS OUT OF IT.

RUTH: Ahhhhhh ...

JACOB: Ruth, what is going on with your speech?

RUTH: I might need an operation on my mouth, Jacob.

JACOB: It's a week now and it's getting worse. If you're working on something I want to help. Why is this happening?

RUTH: (pause) Are we ever going to move?

JACOB: Where do you want to move to?

*IN THE DISTANCE IS HEARD THE SOUND
OF A TRAIN WHISTLE, MOURNFUL,
HAUNTING, BEAUTIFUL. OUT OF IT GROWS
THE SOUNDS OF THE ANGEL CHOIR,
LARGO MYSTERIOSO. JACOB IS UNAWARE
OF THE SOUND. RUTH IS ENTRANCED.*

RUTH: To the tower ... the tower ...

*JACOB FADES AWAY AND RUTH IS
ISOLATED.*

RUTH: I want to build. I want to build a tower
whose top reaches unto heaven. A tower so
high that when I stand at the top and look
down a palm tree below will seem no larger
than a grasshopper. I dream of building and I
build of dreaming. I am the woman of brick,
embedded in this tower of brick, baked hard
and laid with slime. I will always live in these
bricks. Even after they decompose I will hover
above this site and trace in ghostly memories
the endless repetition of the bricks. I love the
bricks, baked hard and burned to a burning.
Each brick bearing its own story. This is the
brick that is laid as the hawk swoops, and this
is the brick that is laid as the mortar runs dry,
and this is the brick that is laid as a wracking
cough seizes the chest. And I live in each one.
I am the woman of the bricks. I'm building the

tower because when it cracks the gates of heaven then every story of every brick will be released at once.

The Bedouin Dance
Reprise

SEVEN BEDOUINS ENTER DANCING. A HARNESS DROPS IN AND FLIES RUTH ABOVE THE DANCING BEDOUINS. THEY PITCH A TENT IN THE MIDDLE OF THE ROOM. WINDS WHIP THE FLAPS. THE ROOM IS COVERED WITH IMAGES OF PALM TREES. IMAGES OF TRAINS CROSSFADE— LONG CAMEL TRAINS AND EARLY NINETEENTH CENTURY LOCOMOTIVES. AS THE BEDOUINS LEAD RUTH FROM HER FLYING POSITION ONTO THE OPERATING TABLE, THEY ARE ECLIPSED BY THE SURGEONS.

The Operating Theatre

RAFEL: What's the pressure?

AMEK: Eighty over fifty—dropping.

ZABI: Change the anesthetic. Stabilize her. Fast!

RAFEL: Scalpel. No! Not that one!

AMEK: Tubing in ... Suction.

RAFEL: X-ray shows the shadow here.

ZABI: No, look at the CAT scan. It's deeper.

RAFEL: Lost it. Vital signs.

AMEK: Pulse getting rapid. Respirations ... twenty-two ...

ZABI: Losing a lot of blood.

RAFEL: Transfuse one unit.

ZABI: She's not going to make it.

RAFEL: Transfuse the unit goddammit!

ZABI: Still losing.

RAFEL: Transfuse second unit ... Add ...

ZABI: Adding!

AMEK: Ligate?

RAFEL: NO! Pressure?

AMEK: Dropping seventy over forty. Ligate?

RAFEL: NO! Now back off! Scalpel.

JACOB: (rushing to her side) Breathe deep,
breathe deep, that's it.

*THE OPERATING TABLE TILTS AND RISES
TO AN UNREAL HEIGHT.*

RUTH: The scene is an operating theatre. I am on
the table. Dreaming.

JACOB: The scene is an operating theatre. I am on
the dreaming.

ZABI: The scene is a table. I am the dreaming.

AMEK: The scene is a dreaming.

RAFEL: The scene is on the dreaming table
dreaming table dreaming.

RUTH, JACOB, RAFEL, AMEK, ZABI:
(absolute unison) I am on the table. Dreaming.

*A WEAVING CHORALE OF GROWING
EXCITEMENT.*

RUTH: I am	JACOB: The scene is
on the table	an operating
dreaming.	theatre

RAFEL: I am on on the table

AMEK: The scene is a dreaming.

ZABI: I am the dreaming.

RUTH: I am on the table dreaming.

JACOB: The scene is an operating theatre

RAFEL: I am on the table.

AMEK: The scene is a dreaming.

ZABI: I am the dreaming.

RUTH: Dreaming.

JACOB: The scene is.

RAFEL: On the table dreaming table dreaming.

AMEK: Dreaming.

ZABI: I am.

RUTH: I am.

JACOB: (delayed) I am.

AMEK: Dreaming.

RUTH: I am.

RAFEL: (delayed) I am.

AMEK: Dreaming.

RUTH: I am.   AMEK: (delayed) I am.

RAFEL: Dreaming.

RUTH: I am.   ZABI: (delayed) I am.

RUTH, JACOB, RAFEL, AMEK, ZABI:
Dreaming.

RUTH: I   JACOB: I

RAFEL: I

AMEK: I   ZABI: I

DRIVING AGITATO.

RAFEL: I hear my heart beating, booming in my
ears.

AMEK: I hear the sound of the scalpel cutting my
flesh.

RUTH: Jacob! The doctors are all speaking with
my voice.

JACOB: Yes ... my voice ...

RUTH: No! My voice.

AMEK: You have many voices.

RUTH: All my voices.

AMEK: We are your many voices.

SPEAKING IN UNISON.

RUTH, JACOB, RAFEL, AMEK, ZABI: We are
your many voices.

PAUSE.

RUTH: All my voices.

PAUSE.

ZABI: Speaking at once.

RUTH: All my   JACOB: Divided
Voices.

RAFEL: All my   AMEK: Voices

        ZABI: Speaking at once.

RUTH, JACOB, RAFEL, AMEK, ZABI: Ohhhh!

RUTH: Oh my God, you're all speaking my mind.
I must be dying!

RAPID ECHOES, LIKE DOMINOS.

JACOB: Dying.

RAFEL: Dying.

AMEK: Dying.

ZABI: Dying.

COUNTERPOINT OF DECAYS AND CRESTS.

RUTH: Dying   JACOB: Dying

RAFEL: Dying   AMEK: Dying

　　　ZABI: Dying

AMEK: If you want to live, concentrate!

RUTH: Ruth, my name is Ruth!

ZABI: There's no need to fear, you never lose your name.

JACOB: The letters that make the name are set in bone.

RUTH: I am my name and when I drift it will anchor me.

AMEK: What will the pain be like when the scalpel cuts?

ZABI: Am I curious?

AMEK: My nerves are screaming.

RUTH: Will I ever stop climbing the face of this tower?

RAFEL: Is the face of this tower malignant?

AMEK: No! It's an open face yearning for paradise.

RAFEL: No! A tower is a tower.

RUTH: I'm sure it's all a mistake—must've used the wrong word.

JACOB: But when?

RAFEL: At the pinnacle.

AMEK: Am I at the top of the tower?

RUTH: (firm and strangely assured) NO. When I reach the top of the tower I will hear the sound of a distant train.

RAFEL: I remember that. How do I remember that?

AMEK: Have I been here before?

ZABI: Oh yes. Many times.

RAFEL: You could almost say you've always been here, like a moth circling a flame.

ZABI: You keep diving into the flame and immolating yourself.

RAFEL: That's why you're on the operating table.

RAFEL, AMEK, ZABI, JACOB: Don't you remember?

HYSTERICALLY GRASPING AT STRAWS.

RUTH: I'll tell the nurse I'm weeping for my memory, not the pain—I'll remember—resist the flame as I circle ... (pause) But in what language?

AMEK: What language am I speaking?

ZABI: Can I move my mouth?

RAFEL: Can I make my mouth migrate?

AMEK: Which way is the tower?

DRIVING AGITATO.

RAFEL: Follow the heat.

ZABI: Always remember that.

RAFEL: Follow the heat. Move towards the heat.
But do not burn yourself.

JACOB: Move   RAFEL: Follow

AMEK: To the heat. ZABI: The heat.

RAFEL: And keep moving. Stay in motion.

JACOB: Forget the doctor, forget your amnesia,
keep moving.

RAFEL: When in trouble speed up and bare your
teeth.

AMEK: Or sing a Requiem for the heat.

GREGORIAN CHANT.

RAFEL, AMEK, ZABI, JACOB: Sanctus, Sanctus,
Sanctus.

LONG PAUSE.

RUTH: It is so still.

JACOB: Listen! Do you hear that sound? Is it the voice of God?

RUTH: (jubilant) It's the sound of a distant train.

The Prison

RUTH'S NIGHTMARE RECURS, THRUSTING HER INTO A PRISON YARD WHERE A RADIO BROADCAST IS BLARING.

The London Times. Dateline Belfast. The Irish Republican Army is engulfed in a serious internal dispute because its most ruthless unit has refused the leadership's order to disband. The renegade unit coordinated the bombing of the annual memorial service for soldiers killed in the two World Wars at Enniskillen in County Fermanagh. The attack killed eleven civilians and provoked worldwide condemnation of the guerillas.

IN THE BACKGROUND IS HEARD THE SOUND OF RIOTS AND THE BABEL TEXT FROM GENESIS IN GAELIC. RUTH WITNESSES PRISONERS CROSS THE YARD CARRYING THEIR PRISON BARS BEFORE THEM. THEY SING.

The Prisoner's Song

We are prisoners on this globe
Condemned alive like Job.
That's why we agree
On the ideology
Of bricks and bitumen.
Building, building, building, is our destiny.
From constant war and chaos we long to be free

SCENE 3

**THE IDEOLOGY OF BRICKS AND
BITUMEN**

<u>**The House**</u>

*AS JACOB ENTERS, RUTH IS ROLLING A
BABYLONIAN BRICK KILN ACROSS THE
STAGE, THICK SMOKE POURING OUT ITS
CHIMNEY.*

JACOB: Ruth, why do I keep finding bricks in
the oven?

RUTH: I thought we could use some more
roughage in our diet, dear.

JACOB: Does this have anything to do with your
obsession with that tower?

RUTH: No, for God's sake, no. Don't worry. I forgot all about that. (directly to the audience as co-conspirators) They're not sun dried bricks but substantial kiln-fired bricks of great durability.

JACOB: Who are you talking to? Are you hearing voices?

RUTH: No, no, just chatting with my guardian angel, darling.

JACOB: There's something veiled about your tone, and there's got to be over two thousand bricks out there.

THE SOUND OF AN ANGEL CHOIR IS HEARD.

RUTH: (entranced) One thousand, nine hundred and ninety-six.

The Brick Dance

BABYLONIAN WORKERS ENTER WITH HODS OF BRICKS AND THE BRICK DANCE BEGINS, WEAVING FLOWING PATTERNS WITH THE BRICKS.

The Operating Theatre

RAFEL: Vital signs.

AMEK: Stabilized.

RAFEL: She's passed the crisis. You've got to leave.

JACOB: I'm staying.

RAFEL: Our policy doesn't—

JACOB: I'm not leaving her.

ZABI: He seems to help her.

AMEK: I agree, absolutely.

RAFEL: All right then—for now.

PAUSE.

JACOB: Her eye motion's so rapid—why?

RUTH'S REALITY INTERSECTS WITH THAT OF THE SURGEONS.

RUTH: I'm at the top of the tower.

AMEK: This anesthetic's giving her dreams.

RUTH: No. I'm in the "room ... one ... passes ... through."

JACOB: I see.

RUTH: Built of blue bricks inlaid with bulls and dragons. The bulls are yellow with manes of lapis lazuli and the dragons white and crested with a shimmering light.

JACOB: It seems she's trying to leave the table.

RUTH: Hold me ... I'm frightened!

ZABI: Secure the restraints.

RUTH: Jacob!

JACOB: Her eyes are ...

HE'S TOO MESMERIZED TO FINISH. THE TWO REALITIES BEGIN TO BLUR.

RUTH: Like black pearls ...

JACOB, RAFEL, AMEK, ZABI: You're talking crazy—stop it! Please!

RUTH: Oh Jacob, I don't want to die!

JACOB, RAFEL, AMEK: You're not!

RUTH: Please tell the Doctor, tell her.

JACOB, AMEK: We know, we're doing everything, it'll be over soon, just hang on.

RUTH: I love you.

RUTH: I love you.   JACOB: Love

RAFEL: Love   AMEK: You

     ZABI: You.

JACOB: I know, Love, I love you, just hang on, breathe deep, breathe deep, that's it.

SUDDENLY THEY ARE STRUCK BY A REVOLUTIONARY FERVOR AS IF THEY WERE IN A SECRET MEETING OF A RADICAL CELL PLANNING A REVOLT.

RAFEL: And they said to one another.

RUTH: Is my mouth burning?

AMEK: Burning.

RAFEL: Why do we not move from this desert?

AMEK: It's not a desert.

RUTH: It's my mouth.

RAFEL: And it's storming heaven.

RUTH: Who is speaking?

RAFEL, AMEK, ZABI, JACOB: If build we do not, then burnt we will be.

RUTH: Yes!

RAFEL, AMEK, ZABI, JACOB: And they said to one another:

RUTH: Yes!

RAFEL, AMEK, ZABI, JACOB: Rise up!

RUTH: Yes.

RAFEL, AMEK, ZABI, JACOB: Rise Up!

RUTH: YES!

ZABI: Build a tower.

RUTH, JACOB, RAFEL, AMEK, ZABI: YES!

RUTH: My mouth is a kiln.

RAFEL, ZABI: I hear the bricks sing as they rise up.

AMEK, JACOB: And the right of revolt—

RUTH: Is embedded in the tower of my mouth.

The Prison

The New York Times. Dateline Lima. A clash in the Upper Huallaga River Valley of Peru has left 15 guerillas of the leftist Shining Path movement and two soldiers dead, the army reported today. Nearly 20,000 people have died in this seemingly endless struggle.

IN THE BACKGROUND IS HEARD THE BABEL TEXT IN A PERUVIAN DIALECT. THE PRISONERS WALK THE YARD, ANGRY AND JOSTLING. TRAPPING RUTH AGAINST THE BARS THEY FORCE A UNIFORM UPON HER. THEY SING.

The Uniform Song

We're caught in every corner of this earth.
We're forced to wear these uniforms from birth.
We're from Belfast and Nicaragua,
Johannesburg, Miami, and the Gaza.
We have no means to profit
And so our lives are forfeit
In the archipelago corporate.

SCENE 4

A TOWER WITH ITS TOP IN THE HEAVENS

The House

JACOB: Can you imagine a conspiracy to take over heaven? You'd have to have meetings, and codes, and secret handshakes ...

RUTH: What are you driving at, Jacob?

JACOB: You ever think about that sort of stuff?

RUTH: I think the amount of conspiracy reported in daily life is vastly exaggerated.

JACOB: Well ... would you happen to be harboring any secret plans?

RUTH: WHAT THE HELL IS GOING ON HERE? YOU FIND SOME LONG DONG SILVER DOLL IN THE CLOSET, OR WHAT?!!!

JACOB: Now hold on, dear, I'm not accusing you of anything. I just got this feeling there's something you're thinking I don't know about ...

RUTH: Of course, I have a secret life. Everyone
has a secret life. For Christ sakes it's only natural.
Some people have plenty of 'em. Now bugger off!

JACOB: All right, Ruth, I'll be in the garden if
there's anything you want to talk about.

*AFTER RUTH IS SURE HE'S GONE SHE
STARTS LAUGHING. AT FIRST SHE'S JUST
CHUCKLING ABOUT HER WORD PLAY BUT
SOON SHE'S OUT OF CONTROL.*

RUTH: Bugger off, that's a good one, Yah ha ha,
bugger...off, Ya Ha,
Buh Ga..Roo, Yo, HO, HA, HO, HA,
BOO GA ROOO NEE, YA, YA, YA, YA, YA, YA,
YA YA,
(scared to death)
JACOB!!!!!

The Operating Theatre

JACOB AND THE SURGEONS ENTER, EACH WITH THEIR OWN OPERATING TABLE ON WHEELS, AND CAROM LIKE BUMPER CARS AROUND THE OPERATING ROOM, SPINNING RUTH WITH THEM.

GIDDY JOKING PUNNING EROTIC EUPHORIC BADINAGE.

RAFEL: The scene's an operating theatre. I'm on the table. Laughing at my fears.

RUTH: I hear my heart beating, booming in my ears.

AMEK: I hear the scalpel cutting my flesh.

RUTH: I hear all my voices focus and mesh.

ZABI: I hear conversations.

RAFEL: Altercations of the surgeons and their nations.

RUTH: Everything I hear is building a tower over my head.

RAFEL: Paradise at the pinnacle.

RAFEL, AMEK: And the tower grows higher.

RAFEL, AMEK, JACOB: As I climb in sweet dread.

RUTH: You won't catch me thinking twice, I'm climbing to Paradise.

CHASING RIDDLES.

ZABI: It seems that the wind is getting louder, or is it the high whine of a drill? The wild and woesome whine of a winter wind whipping through the weaving wheel.

AMEK: "W!" Is the answer in the letter "W?"

RUTH: "W" West, we wander ..."L" Listen, to my lungs laboring ... "D" Dying. Am I dying?

RAFEL: Of course I'm dying.

ZABI: And I've died many times before.

RAFEL: "T" Time, counting the pulse.

AN EROTICON.

RAFEL: My throbbing heart.

AMEK: So warm.

ZABI: So sticky.

JACOB: So exciting.

RUTH: So vibrating, like a hummingbird in the genitals.

RUTH: You won't catch me thinking twice, I'm climbing to Paradise.

RAPID-FIRE CAPRICCIO.

AMEK: Is the doctor speaking Babel?

ZABI: Who, that one?

RAFEL: The funny one.

JACOB: She's singing in Greek she's at the peak.

RUTH: She's teasing me!

RAFEL: She's building the walls of the tower.

AMEK: Is the tower evil?

JACOB: It's a glorious thing.

RAFEL: Like a pinnacle of flame.

JACOB: Around which we huddle, eon after eon.

RAFEL: A point of flame.

ZABI: Flame baking brick, building breathtaking "B."

RUTH, JACOB, RAFEL, AMEK, ZABI: Building, building, building.

AMEK: BREATH. Don't forget to breathe.

RUTH: Me?

RAFEL: No, you.

AMEK: You comic Sumerians.

ZABI: Babel on, Babylon.

RUTH: You won't catch me thinking twice, I'm climbing to Paradise.

VOLUPTUOUS AND ABANDONED.

RUTH: If I die, I die lost in the alphabet.

AMEK: Swimming and swooning in sweat.

ZABI: If in space or in mind.

RUTH: No tongue has defined.

AMEK: And if the Tower's in my mind, can I hide it from the Lord?

HOLY ROLLING REVELATIONS.

RUTH: Is that Him behind that blue mask?

ZABI: Mask! Yes! "M," the mastical mystical musical mask of "M."

RUTH: Oh my God, I'm being born again and there's bricks everywhere!

LUSH AND SLOW.

ZABI: And the music is so sweet.

RAFEL: This sound. All these sounds.

AMEK: They drew me here. They break my heart.

ZABI: The music.

JACOB: Swept on elocusic currents of music.

RAFEL: The music cuts to the bone and sets me free.

JACOB: Ain't no lies in the bones.

RAFEL: In the free fall of the bones lies the song of an alphabet.

AMEK: The language of my body.

RUTH: The babel of my body.

RUTH: You won't catch me thinking twice, I'm climbing to Paradise.

TIME TRAVELING.

RUTH HEARS THE ANGEL CHOIR ECHOING IN THE WHISTLE OF A DISTANT TRAIN. SHE WRAPS HERSELF IN A HUGE AZURE VEIL THAT DROPS DOWN FROM THE GRID AND FILLS THE STAGE, ITS LINES COMING TO A FOCUS AT HER FACE. THE OTHERS FADE AWAY. SHE WILLS HERSELF INTO A TIME-TRANCE AND TRAVELS TO ANCIENT BABYLON. SHE ENTERS THE LIFE OF ONE OF THE ORIGINAL TOWER BUILDERS AND ADDRESSES A POWERFUL JUDGE, HOPING TO FIND FORGIVENESS.

I hear the siren voices of the Tower. The wild beauty of millions of voices drawing me into their labors. And in labor I labor, no time for childbirth, just drop the infant into the apron and back, climbing back, to the beacon. The ascending steps are on the East. The descending steps on the West. One year to the top. If a man falls, if a woman falls, if a child falls, we grieve, quietly, but we do not stop. But if a brick falls we weep, for a brick takes a year to replace. There are whole seasons when the clouds turn an ominous blood red. Perhaps a warning to those among us whose ambition is as dark. It is my fervent wish to ascend to heaven simply to dwell there. But there are those who labor by my side whose intention it is to ascend and serve idols and there are even those who are climbing to wage war with God. Perhaps their cause is just. I know I feel a knot in my throat when they cry the Ancient One slaughtered the entire earth with His flood and we must revolt or we will be His victims again and again. They constantly shoot arrows toward heaven, which, when returning, are seen to be covered with blood. They cry, "We have slain all who are in heaven," but I know they are deluded. I believe that the crafty warrior we are approaching is fortifying their delusions so that He will have the advantage of surprise. Already I have seen evidence of His strategy. My work prospers. I go to lay a brick and two are laid. I go to mortar a row and two are mortared. But those around me falter. The men and women who would worship idols are subject to strange maladies. Some turn into apes and run scrambling and screeching up and down the scaffolding overturning vats of mortar and hods of brick. Others suffer a horrible plague. Puffing and bloating into strange shapes like inflated goat bladders they lift off the tower and are blown away by the wind. Still I climb. Brick after brick. Climbing, climbing. My hands are a permanent red from the beautiful bricks burned to a burning. And still I climb. A woman that I worked alongside happily for years is gone now. I had said to her, I need more mortar, and she, like a beast, bellowed these sounds—Please believe me, I know you must think I am mad to suggest something without meaning, but these were the sounds I heard—rafel mahee amek zabi almit. Since it was impossible that she did not understand me, I repeated my words, and she lunged at me with a brick. I snapped her neck. Nothing will prevent me from reaching heaven.

The Prison

The New York Times. Dateline Johannesburg. Three men have been arrested in connection with the massacre of twenty-six black passengers on a commuter train, South Africa's Law and Order Ministry said today. The Ministry stated that the massacre stems from the battle for supremacy between the African National Congress and the Zulu organization, Inkatha, during which nearly eight hundred people have been killed.

*IN THE BACKGROUND IS HEARD THE BABEL
TEXT CHANTED IN BANTU. THE PRISONERS
DO A MORBID DANCE WITH THEIR BARS, AND
SING.*

The Song of Walls

They're building more walls
In our invisible prison halls
Than the naked eye can see
Spinning outside spinning inside
Spinning inside spinning outside
Money's the great divide

SCENE 5

VICTORY CLIMBING INTO THE JAWS OF DEFEAT

The House

JACOB: So here I am itchin' to do some of my own climbing. Yes, I'm a climber, climbing, climbing, too. And I got my snout sewn into the clouds sniffing for a clue that'll launch me. And I come across this one Yahoo who says that to get really high you first have to get down, so I found myself in the Inferno. We're goin' lower and lo and behold we came upon a giant bellowing a chant, RAFEL MAHEE AMEK ZABI ALMIT, and Virgil told Dante this was Nimrod, the king who built the Tower of Babel. Nimrod, oh yes, Nimrod. And so he's condemned to forever babble nonsense, babble babble babble nonsense. It was then I realized the danger that Ruth is in.

RUTH: Jacob! It's happening! Oh Lord, Oh Hashem, Oh Yahweh, don't do ... it ...
Rafel mahee amek zabi almit
Rafel mahee amek zabi almit
Rafel mahee amek zabi almit

*JACOB SCRAMBLES FOR "THE INFERNO"
AND INTONES VIRGIL'S TAUNT OF*

NIMROD TO EXORCISE RUTH. SHE CHANTS
UNTIL HE BREAKS THE CURSE.

JACOB: "Began a bellowed chant from her
brute mouth!"

RUTH: Jacob, *rafel* how *maheee* can you *amek* be
so *zabi almit*?!

JACOB: "Babbling fool, stick to your horn and
vent yourself with it when rage or passion stir
your stupid soul."

RUTH: You *amek*, you lousy *almit mahee*, how
dare *rafel amek*!

JACOB: "Feel there around your neck, you
muddle-head, and find the horn there on your
overgrown chest!"

RUTH: Keep your smutty mouth off my chest! Oh
Lord! Jacob! It stopped.

JACOB: Please forgive me, darling, but if I don't
make you angry you don't snap out of it.

RUTH: How dare you call me stupid! I have a
condition.

JACOB: That's an understatement. You're a
goddamn walking Tower of Babel.

RUTH AND JACOB MISS LIKE SHIPS IN THE NIGHT.

JACOB: Pass the milk, please.

RUTH: Do you want bitumen for your toast?

LONG PAUSE.

JACOB: Bitumen?

LONG PAUSE.

RUTH: What?

LONG PAUSE.

JACOB: Bitumen. You said bitumen.

RUTH: What's a bitumen?

JACOB: I don't know, you said it.

SHE STORMS OUT AND HE YELLS TO HER DEPARTING BACK.

JACOB: Why won't you trust me? You're not the only one with a secret life!

*BUT RUTH HAS ALREADY GONE. AN
IMPOSSIBLY HIGH LADDER APPEARS IN THE
CENTER OF THE LIVING ROOM. AROUND IT
THE CLOUDS ARE SWIRLING IN ALL THE HUES
OF THE SUNSET. SILENT BEDOUINS GLIDING
OUT OF THE WINGS MYSTERIOUSLY GUIDE
JACOB TO THE BASE OF THE LADDER.*

I want to climb my ladder. I am afraid of falling.
But I love to climb. When I climb I enter God's
country. When I climb the air shimmers. When I
climb I fuse with the horizon, flatten right out and
wrap around three sixty. When I climb my neck
prickles and my hackles tickle. When I climb I get
that creepy crawly formicative pruriginously itchy
sense sensation. When I climb I dream of
cornucopic compendiums of corpulent Coptic
concubines. Jack in motherfuckers and let's go!

To climb one must know the rungs. Some portion
of the brain sends a thought impulse to the nerves,
which goose the muscles and the leg rises. How
high it rises depends on your nerves. If you've got
a lot of nerve it goes real high. One, and I mean
one, never knows how high is high enough, but
that is never the issue when one, and I mean one,
is climbing. To climb one must know the terrain
and the terrain is voices—once above the clouds
you gotta keep your ears peeled for voices, there's
millions of them, but whether you can grab one
and sing it clean is not a cut and dry question.

First of all, you hafta watch out for God cause the son ofa bitch'll swoop right outa the azure and blindside ya—ram ya just like some battle-barge in Nero's floatin' circus. Sometimes he rides a great bird like an Albatross, yellin' like Goddam Idi Amin. And sometimes he strafes you from an ancient test aircraft in his Chuck Yeager outfit screamin profanities like "Git outa my envelope you withered tuber." And sometimes he drifts in on these weird figures that look like bloated goat bladders with gleaming golden eyes. If you get clipped by one of those babies you drop like a rock.

So as I said, it's a matter of getting to know the rungs. You gotta get real close to them. Maybe set up a workshop in your dwelling, your shelter, whatever the hell you call it, I don't give a monkey's dick, words are nothin' to me, wherever it is you live, and you might not live in your house, I'm trying to say something here about where it is you really live, and I can't come right out and say it because HE: Idi Chuck Yaweh, might be up there listening and he doesn't always stay up there in his lurid little costume dramas. Sometimes he comes down here and mucks about where the people live, so where you live is something you need to play pretty close to the chest.

Now in your workshop you get tight to these rungs. So when you're climbing so high and you caught a voice and you're soaring and those harmonic dissonances are swirling round and the angels are all casting lots to see who's gonna get the first shot at ya, then you're locked in solid to your rungs. You know where you are. Your feet and this object have a magnetic attraction like the two halves of the horizon. You got that groove and you and your ladder are smokin'. Rungs are flying by so fast that even the angels trying to grab on are bein thrown off like hobos missin' stride on a fast freight. The angels recover instantly and the next thing they'll do is flood the airwaves with mirages.

Their favorite is the Tower of Babel. Beautiful thing. Sight set me reeling first time they sprung it on me. And the sound of those millions of human voices all singin' in unison, an ode to joy that made all my nerves flow like the muddy Missisip, just flat out wet myself right there, ejaculated, bled from my ears, the ninety percent of my body that is water reclaimed itself right there, the amphibians crawled back into the sea and the sea rewrote the history right there. But that's just to set you up, because when you're staring at the pinnacle of this tower—your eyeballs a liquid mass—the lightning bolt comes out of some theatrical cloud and shatters every voice in a hundred shards. And all of a sudden it's

Swahili and Chinese and Croatian and Balinese
and Babylonian and Yoruba and Lithuanian and
Portuguese and Sicilian and Mongolian and
Finnish and Danish and Zulu and Estonian and
Gaelic and your throat seizes up and you blow out
like shrapnel tracing cartwheels in seventeen
directions like those deadly five pointed throwing
disks you see in Bruce Lee movies. They
confiscate your ladder. Piles of them in heaven's
pound. The memory of your ladder song is
something you can't find even if you sift through
every Korean deli in Harlem, every pizza joint in
Little Italy, every bodega in Hell's Kitchen.

Tap in tight again here because I'm between the
lines again: Advice on where to pick up memory's
shards is harder to come by than God's grace. You
see, scuttlebutt scutts it, hearsay hints it, rumor
rags it that when one looks on the ruins of this
tower one forgets everything one knows. My wife
RUTH has resolved that the only way to overcome
this horrible confusion of tongues is to secretly
rebuild the tower. She thinks that I don't know of
her plan. She's even more secretive than I am, but
I discovered her dream because of the very porous
state of mind that floats over our heads as we
sleep. And secretly, I wish her Godspeed.
Because when she succeeds in constructing her
new Tower brick by brick within her mind and
then springs it full blown, full built, then the Lord,
the goddam landlord of the envelope, will be

forced to come to the table. Forced to negotiate. We want to be in Paradise. We want it. We deserve it. You bet your ass, it's Hubris. And about time. How many millennium we gonna scrape around the humble pen? You heard the story? Said it himself, "Behold, they are one people, and they all have one language; and nothing they propose to do will now be impossible for them." Hear that?!!!!! Do you hear that? Anything we can imagine, we can do. Well, I say, tap in, jack in, and get tight with those rungs, because I'm ready to climb.

A SQUADRON OF ANGELS DIVE BOMBS JACOB, AND, LIKE A FLYING WALLENDA, HE EVADES EACH WAVE. RUTH RETURNS, DICTIONARY IN HAND, UNAWARE OF THE ANGELS, AND IS ALARMED BY JACOB'S BEHAVIOR.

RUTH: Jacob! What are you doing!

THE ANGELS EXIT, WINGS TWITCHING WITH ANNOYANCE.

JACOB: Nothing dear, just chatting with my guardian angels.

RUTH: I found it. "Bitumen" — it's tar or asphalt, earthy pitchy stuff, mortar.

JACOB: Didn't you tell me this once before?

RUTH: When? (now alarmed) When?

The Operating Theatre

RAFEL: Check the respirator.

ZABI: She's starting to come to. Increase anesthetic.

AMEK: Increased.

JACOB: Breathe deep, breathe deep, that's it.

ZABI: Taking it in.

RAFEL: Eyes glazed.

ZABI: She's under again.

SHE'S FALLING UNCONSCIOUS, LIGHTLY, SOFTLY.

RUTH: Falling.

RUTH, JACOB, RAFEL, AMEK, ZABI: The tower rises.

RUTH: Falling.

AMEK: Neck bristles.

RUTH: Falling.

RAFEL: Sweet sweat.

ZABI: Wet sweet wet.

RUTH, JACOB, RAFEL, AMEK, ZABI: The tower rises.

RUTH: Where's my body?

AMEK: Sweet body.

RAFEL: Sweat body.

ZABI: Falling bodies.

RUTH, JACOB, RAFEL, AMEK, ZABI: The tower rises.

RUTH: Rising.

RUTH, JACOB, RAFEL, AMEK, ZABI: Rising.

RUTH: Rising.

NOW THAT SHE'S COMPLETELY UNDER, A VIOLENT ARGUMENT BEGINS.

ZABI: An operating theatre. I am on the table.

RUTH: I am on the table!

ZABI: Yes, on the table.

RUTH: Stop taking my voice!

ZABI: We're all the same voice.

RUTH: No! It's a trap!

RAFEL: Where am I?

RUTH: Is this a prison?

ZABI: There's no way out!

RAFEL: Kabul? Sarajevo?

RUTH: How do I do that How do they do that
How do I do that How do they ...

AMEK: (as RUTH repeats) How do I do that How
do they do that.

RUTH: As fast as thought.

RAFEL: I hear my thoughts in other mouths.

AMEK: My mouth is disappearing.

RAFEL: We lose the West Bank we'll be destroyed.

JACOB: No. Leveraged buyouts are good for the economy.

RUTH: Then who put me in this cell?

JACOB: False prophets.

RAFEL: False profits.

RUTH: I remember that.

RAFEL: How do I remember that?

JACOB: It's a convulsion.

AMEK: A takeover boom.

RUTH: I want out I want out I want out I want out I want out.

ZABI: She's not going to make it.

RAFEL: Transfer the unit, goddammit!

RUTH: I need more mortar.

JACOB: Slam the cell, it's the SEC.

JACOB, ZABI: Rafel mahee amek zabi almit.

RUTH: I'm gonna break out, I'm gonna break out!

ZABI: There's no way out that way!

RUTH: You're wrong!

RUTH, JACOB, AMEK, RAFEL: WE BREAK
NOW!

SUDDENLY, RUTH IS ISOLATED IN THE LIGHT.
EVERYONE ELSE FADES AWAY.

RUTH: How I was born to this cell I'll never know,
but all of a sudden there I was, the striped suit, the
blaring klaxons—Arrooogah, Arroogah, and those
leering German Shepherds. It coulda been
anywhere, I didn't know, so I started watching the
way the water went down the drain. That would
at least give me the right hemisphere, but I
realized I was already entirely in the right
hemisphere and the water rushing down always
made me think of God. And it very well coulda
been God who kept changing the sound outside
the walls. Sometimes it sounded tropical like it
coulda been San Salvador. And sometimes I heard
this hot desert wind and it coulda been Baghdad.
When I was nightshipped in I was unconscious so
I figure my disorientation is Someone's idea of
strategic. I see no one. Occasionally I hear shrieks

from what must be other prisoners, but I never decipher their languages. Words drift in through the food slot on all kinds of voices. Barrel chested meat butchers, the divas cackling in Mozart's Prague, the eunuchs in the seraglio—greed oozing from every one of their vowels, even an odd angel or two snagged in the wax (they whisper that in the beginning there were only consonants—and God's gift to Man in the garden was vowels—The Lord giveth and the Lord laugheth all the way to the bank—try laughing without vowels). What are the stories they're trying to tell? There's the one with the file in the cake, there's the one about the gun out of soap, there's the one about hiding inside the corpse. Every story they sing ends in death so every night in my cell, not that I know when night folds me in its iron maiden's bosom— lights always flashing in here like a pinball morgue—I plan my escape. I'm building a tower and climbing out. Every night, all night, I scratch the bricks of the cell. Hardening my nails for the climbing.

The Prison

The Wall Street Journal. Dateline the Gaza Strip. A Palestinian youth was killed and thirty-eight others were wounded as Arab residents of the West Bank and Gaza Strip struck to protest a surge of killings by Israeli

troops acting under tough measures to quell
the uprising called the Intifadah.

IN THE BACKGROUND IS HEARD THE
BABEL TEXT IN ARABIC. THE PRISONERS
ATTEMPT TO BREAK OUT. STANDING ON
TOP OF EACH OTHER'S SHOULDERS THEY
TRY TO SCALE THE BARS. THEY SING.

The Break Out Song

All we want is to break out
of the bondage of money and doubt!

SCENE 6

THE BOOK OF SLIPPAGE

The House

RUTH: Jacob, I want you to play Nimrod.

JACOB: What is this, some new sex fantasy?

RUTH: No, I need help on my project, but I
can't explain. Not yet.

JACOB: Just what is this project, Ruth? Is it
connected to the government?

RUTH: If I let the idea out of my own mind there'll be leaks.

JACOB: I can keep a secret.

RUTH: I know you can. It's not that you would say anything, it's ... slippage.

JACOB: Slippage?

RUTH: Yes, you remember my last project, *The Book of Slippage*? Things get in the air, then like in aerodynamics they develop resistance and accidents happen, a constant slipstream of accidents. So forgive me, but I'm not letting anything into the air. I'm going to be my own wind tunnel.

JACOB: All right, what's my costume? Georgio Armani three-piece? Sharkskin zoot suit? Golden caftan?

RUTH: Ya nailed it on the last one. Nimrod was the King who built the Tower of Babel, the tower of ... yes ... the Tower of ... Babel ... of ...
(stammering)
Ba ... bel
Ba bel
Ba bel
Ba bel

JACOB: Ruth!

The Operating Theatre

AMEK: The heart rate just went sky high.

RAFEL: I don't know what we're looking at here.

ZABI: Her tongue's convulsing!

JACOB: Doctor, I'm shaking all over. What's happening!?

THE OPERATING ROOM EXPLODES LIKE A REVIVALIST MEETING.

RUTH: Nimrod, Nimrod, Nimrod was also the great grandson of Noah.

AMEK: Noah, Noah.

ZABI: And talk about sins of the fathers. The sins of the fathers.

RAFEL: Nimrod's granddaddy Ham came upon his father, Noah.

ZABI: Granddaddy Ham, Granddaddy Ham, Nimrod's Granddaddy Ham.

JACOB: Came upon his father, Noah,

AMEK: Noah, Noah.

JACOB: In the tent, passed out naked in a drunken stupor.

RUTH: Ham went and told his brothers that Dad was hanging out in the tent.

RUTH, JACOB, RAFEL, AMEK, ZABI: Oh Dad, Ohhh Dad was a hanging out.

RUTH: So the two bro took a sheepskin, and laid it upon both their shoulders, and went backwards and covered the nakedness of their father.

JACOB, RAFEL, ZABI: And covered the nakedness, the nakedness, of their father.

RUTH: Now

JACOB: Now

RAFEL: Now

AMEK: Now

ZABI: (screaming) Now!

RUTH: Now the story gets a little murky. It seems that Noah wakes up and realizes that Ham has done something to him, and so he curses Ham's son Canaan to be a slave.

JACOB: A slave   RAFEL: Curses, he curses

AMEK: Ham's son   ZABI: To be. A slave.
Canaan.

RUTH: But what the hell did Ham do wrong?

JACOB: All he did was see his dad naked.

RAFEL: How does Noah know that anything's happened?

AMEK: He got a sore asshole when he was nappin'?

ZABI: This some accusation of incest?

RUTH: Why mince words? Call it like it is.

RUTH: Right here in The Bible is a justification of slavery!

JACOB: Slavery   RAFEL: Slavery

AMEK: Slavery   ZABI: Justification

AMEK: And why?

ZABI: And why?

RAFEL: A punishment for a son seeing his
father naked?

ZABI: What!! How can that be?!

AMEK: Oh it don't really mean *that*.
The Good Book's talkin 'bout incest.

RUTH, JACOB, RAFEL, AMEK: It means
incest, incest, incest.

ZABI: If we sing it as a tale of incest, then it's
really a mangle,
'cause how are we sposed to untangle
the truth when it's veiled, veiled,
veiled in double speak?
O double double speak.

RUTH: So now you know what's brewing in
Nimrod's mind.

RAFEL: The son of a slave.

AMEK: Maybe he wanted revenge.

ZABI: But maybe he was pure of heart
and wanted to wipe all that away

and walk with God again.

RUTH: He began to be a mighty one on the earth.

RAFEL: A mighty one.

RUTH, AMEK: He was a mighty hunter before the Lord.

RAFEL: Before the Lord.

RUTH, AMEK, ZABI: And the beginning of his kingdom was,

RAFEL: The beginning was,

RUTH, JACOB, RAFEL, AMEK, ZABI: (crescendo) Babel Babel Babel!

JACOB: Ruth!

RUTH: Yes?

JACOB: Nothing is gonna be impossible for us now!

RUTH: But beware of slippage and do not speak.

RAFEL: Absolute silence and there'll be no leak.

AMEK, ZABI: A song of silence to the Tower's peak.

The Prison

New York Times. Dateline Srinagar, Kashmir. Indian troops burned down four hundred houses and killed at least twenty people in the town of Handwara, said Indian reporters at the scene. The troops from the paramilitary Border Security Force were said to have been retaliating after a grenade was thrown by a Kashmiri guerilla.

IN THE BACKGROUND IS HEARD THE BABEL TEXT IN HINDI. RUTH'S HEAD IS BOUND BY A BLACK HOOD. THE PRISONERS SING.

The Song of Censorship

We must not speak. We must not see,
Jailor says,
There's only one reality,
Jailor says,
If I want your opinion
I will give it to you.
So we must not speak. We must not see
There's more than one reality.

SCENE 7

SIMOON

<u>The House</u>

RUTH: Do you feel anything?

JACOB: What is that, an invitation to fight?

RUTH: No, no, do you feel a presence, like this strange presence, in the house?

JACOB: No.

RUTH: Don't just dismiss it like that. Give it a chance.

JACOB: I'm sorry. Why don't I see if I can hunt down this ...
(suddenly confounded)
... TOOOOOWWWEERRRR ... OF ... MORTAL COILS ...
No! I'm in BIG trouble making my words COME.
[who is moving my lips?]
EXCEPT IN SIMOONS OF MORTAL COILS.
... DID YOU DO THIS?!!

RUTH: What did you say—you said—
HERE ... COMES ... THE BIG ONE!

*TWISTERS ARE COMING FROM THREE
DIRECTIONS, LIGHTNING FLASHES, AND A
LARGE WHITE FIST FILLS THE AIR. THREE
SMALL CONES OF SAND FORM ACROSS
THE STAGE AS IF HOURGLASSES WERE
DRAINING SLOWLY FROM ABOVE.*

The Operating Theatre

RUTH: I am on the table. Of destruction.

ZABI: Three hundred and forty years of simoons,
sand whipping storms.

JACOB, RAFEL, AMEK, ZABI: What is this wind?

RUTH: Is it the presence of the Lord?

JACOB, RAFEL, AMEK, ZABI: What is this wind?

JACOB: Is it the sound of our language blowing
away?

RUTH: How long must we walk through this
wind before we reach the Doctor's mind?

JACOB: Who is speaking?

RUTH: How can I have lost my way?
How can I have lost my way?

When all I must remember
is to lift my head.
(pause)
Yes, now I can feel my blood memory rushing
back to me.

*AT THE SURFACE THE SURGEONS WARN OF
HEART ATTACK.*

ZABI: Looks like cardiac arrest.

AMEK: Heart rate blue line.

RAFEL: CPR fast. Conductors. Current. Hurry.
Vital signs.

AMEK: None.

RAFEL: Again. Conductors. Current. Vital signs.

AMEK: No movement.

JACOB: KEEP TRYING.

RAFEL: Again. Try it here.

JACOB: Ruth, please, don't die.

RAFEL: Conductors. Up voltage. Current. Vital
signs. Vital signs. Give me vital signs. Damn it!

AMEK: (long pause) None.

PAUSE.

RAFEL: She's gone. We're sorry. We did everything we could. We're sorry.

JACOB: Noooooooooooooo...> (He collapses)

PAUSE.

BACK INSIDE RUTH'S MIND.

RAFEL, AMEK, ZABI: (a clear, meditative tone, sustaining) Ooooooooo ...

RUTH: I am levitating on the table.

RUTH, JACOB: I've been silent for so long I've focused enormous energy.

RUTH, JACOB, RAFEL, AMEK, ZABI: I can feel the thrill coursing through my body, the shivers and tremors.

RUTH: And I start to rise.

RUTH, AMEK: I am above it.

RUTH: Floating above it.

RUTH, ZABI: I can see my body below on the table.

RUTH, RAFEL: I can see a tunnel with a bright white light at the end.

RUTH, JACOB: Or is it a tower?

RUTH, AMEK: I don't know if I am moving up or across. There are no dimensions here.

RUTH: A prayer, my motion is a prayer.

RUTH, ZABI: Drifting in prayer, I catapult and somersault through the air.

RUTH: Almighty God, I love thee.

RUTH LEAVES THE OPERATING TABLE AND STANDS ALONE.

After years of building, brick by brick, I broke through the skin of heaven with my tower. And there, hovering above the pinnacle—about six inches—floating on what looked like the shimmers above asphalt roads in heat waves, was a temple with a hot pink marble gate. I lunged at the gate and there He was—The Lord. A long white man with a long white beard rising from a long white chaise lounge. His eyes were ghosting like black pearls and his teeth ... he broke into a broad grin at the sight of me ... The Teeth ... The Teeth ... were not white but brass. I was dazzled by their razor sharp points and I think He knew they were one of His best features. "Good Evening," He said, "would you care for a cocktail?" "No thank you," I shot back, "I'd rather wrestle." Like an ancient Fred Astaire, He glided across the threshold and clapped me in a full-nelson. I felt his hot breath scorch the back of my neck and I knew every gazelle on the Serengeti ever fallen upon by excellent hyenas. "My angel," He crooned, and I could feel this powerful wraith getting the horn. I slammed my heel down on his foot and he let out a howl like a demon in the Chinese Opera. "Nice move, you flatulent funambulist," I spit, as I snaked out of his grip, "but not yet." I gave him a ramming head butt to the solar plexus, but even as I heard the breath fly out of him he dissolved in a fog and I felt this burning sensation in my ass. Yaweh, the Angry Avenging God, was trying to bugger me in His spirit form. I was thrashing around on twenty-five hot feet desperately trying to clamp down this mist tunneling up my ass. There was only one thing I knew He'd fall for—I'd have to pretend to submit. "Forgive me Lord, I don't know what got into me, Oh Hashem, please set me free and I will worship you." That gets em every time. Pfffffftt—there He was, rubbing His hands like a fly. *Long* fingers. "Now my child," He commanded, "assume the position." I got down on all fours and looking back between my

legs I watched Him approach. Longest shlong I
ever saw, the prime patriarchal part, a real biblical
number. In a flash, I whirled, and one hand
grabbed the frightful head and one hand that
awful wrinkled sack. He exploded with a deadly
babel of curses in Swahili and Chinese and
Croatian, and Balinese and Babylonian and
Yoruba, and Lithuanian and Portuguese and
Sicilian, and Mongolian and Finnish and Danish,
and Zulu and Estonian and Gaelic, and it must
have been my fist clenched around His nuts that
blocked Him from dematerializing because we
started whirling around and around like those hot
desert whirlwinds the Bedouins call simoons. We
got huge, swelling up so big we bloated all five
kingdoms of heaven. Then we'd tornado the other
way, shrinking like water down a drain until the
tear drop of a locust loomed as large as the Dead
Sea. All this time, I don't know if I'm awake or
asleep, I just keep mouthing, "I want to be in
Paradise. I want to be in Paradise. I want to be ..."
I lost track of time. Many times I think I fainted. I
saw visions of nomads moving through the desert
with long camel trains. My mind kept wandering
to the Hanging Gardens and then I'd suffer the
hammering of hundreds of fists, like nomadic
drummers, on my mouth and ears, bruising them
to pulp. Then I heard the sound of a distant train,
mournful, haunting, beautiful—was it the far
voice of God?—and I found myself on the

operating table—Jacob saying, "Breathe deep, breathe deep, that's it ... breathe deep, that's it ..."

The Prison

Wall Street Journal. Dateline Kabul. Afghan guerillas fired a rocket into Kabul killing six people and wounding nineteen.

IN THE BACKGROUND IS HEARD THE BABEL TEXT IN PASHTO. THE OPERATING TABLE HAS RISEN TO A HEIGHT OF SEVEN FEET. THE PRISONERS WRAP IT WITH BARS. RUTH CLAMBERS UP INTO THE SUPPORTS BENEATH THE TABLE. JACOB FOLLOWS. THEY SING.

The Religious Song

Wrestling with the Lord.
A prison of love, death, and discord.

SCENE 8

DISPERSION

The House

RUTH AND JACOB ARE SWINGING UPSIDE DOWN BY THEIR KNEES BENEATH THE TOWERING OPERATING TABLE. THEY'RE ATTEMPTING TO LAUGH SO AS NOT TO

SCREAM. RAFEL, AMEK, AND ZABI STAND IN THE LIVING ROOM LIKE A GREEK CHORUS.

RUTH: Jacob! The house is on fire!

RAFEL, AMEK, ZABI: What is this wind?

JACOB: The garden's a bonfire!

RAFEL, AMEK, ZABI: Rafel mahee amek zabi almit.

RUTH: The television's exploding!

RAFEL, AMEK, ZABI: What is this wind?

JACOB: The toilet's an inferno!

RAFEL, AMEK, ZABI: Rafel mahee amek zabi almit.

RUTH: Look at the pink flamingos! Blazing!

RAFEL, AMEK, ZABI: What is this wind?

RUTH: Jacob, I can't see! The wind's seared my eyes!

RAFEL, AMEK, ZABI: Rafel mahee amek zabi almit. (repeating sotto voce)

JACOB: You hear that riveting sound?!!

RUTH: Oh no, I'm falling ...

JACOB: Every word is shattering into its alphabet.

RUTH: I'm falling ...

JACOB: The air is swirling with jagged D's and razor sharp L's, and boomeranging V's combining with each other more rapidly than words froth in the idiot savant's mouth. An orgy of alphabets cross pollinating, the Hebrew mating with the Greek, the Egyptian hieroglyphic with the Cyrillic.

RUTH: Falling ...

JACOB: When we're hit by this bolt of sound our hearts will burst with the sound of a thousand choirs.

RUTH: The sky blackened with falling bodies.

JACOB: This is the end of the Tower. The end!

RUTH: No! Walk three days in the shadow of the ruins. Meet me at the sound of a distant train.

JACOB: I can't! RUTH! You have to stop!

RUTH: I'm going to build!

The Operating Theatre

AMEK: Doctor, look at this! The heart rate's coming back!

RAFEL: Oh my God, I don't believe it!

JACOB: Yes, yes, please!

ZABI: She's been gone three minutes. It's impossible!

RAFEL: Oxygen fast. We're going in.

RUNNING FROM THE APOCALYPSE

ZABI: I can't hold a thought.

AMEK: As it forms it fades.

RAFEL: The thought breaks.

ZABI: Cracking.

JACOB, AMEK: Running.

JACOB, AMEK, ZABI: They are running.

RUTH, JACOB, RAFEL, AMEK, ZABI: Huge masses running.

RAFEL: Pulsing with voices,
a choir of seventy angels,
all singing as they cast lots
to destroy our tongues.

AMEK: What a divine cacophony.

RUTH: As I wander over the dunes
I see the seventy.
Wandering, wandering,
I see the seventy.

AMEK: An angel to destroy the tongue of
Japheth.

ZABI: An angel to destroy the tongue of Ham.

JACOB: An angel to destroy the tongue of
Shem.

RUTH, JACOB, RAFEL, AMEK, ZABI: Seventy
angels for seventy tongues.

RUTH: I see the seventy
as I wander the ruins
of this scarred and babbling tower.

AVENGING ANGELS STRIDE IN A
CONTINUOUS FILE ACROSS THE STAGE, SOME
OF THEM BATTLE WEARY, SOME WITH

*SWORDS RAISED. THEY TRAVEL THROUGH
THE SHADOWS OF RUINED CITIES LIKE
SARAJEVO, BERUIT, AND POSTWAR BERLIN.*

The Prison

The Chicago Tribune. Dateline Miami.
Violence in Miami ebbed after two nights of
rioting in the mostly black Overtown and
Liberty City areas. The riots touched off by the
fatal shooting of a black motorcyclist by a
Hispanic policeman, highlighted increasing
tensions between the Black and Hispanic ...

*THE OTHER PRISONERS ATTACK RUTH
AND SHE FENDS THEM OFF WITH A
TROWEL. ALONE AND IN DISGUST, SHE
HURLS THE TROWEL TO THE GROUND.*

SCENE 9

BABEL

The House

*RUTH PULLS JACOB INTO THE RUINS OF
THEIR BURNT HOME. THE CHAIRS ARE
STILL SMOLDERING.*

JACOB: Ruth, a third of the house is burnt to the
ground, the back third was swallowed in the

earth, and so what if the living room's still
standing—what the hell are we doing here?!

RUTH: In this room will rise the new Tower of
Babel. Please, come with me.

JACOB: That tower is in ruins and its builder is
buried to the waist in the eighth circle. For god's
sake, break off this insane plan.

RUTH: I have rebuilt it.

JACOB: Whoever looks upon those ruins forgets
everything they know.

RUTH: What?

JACOB: Ruth?

RUTH: What?

JACOB: Ruth! Speak to me!

*SHE STARTS A DRONING MESMERIZING
CHANT.*

RUTH: Walk for three days in the shadow of the
tower,
three days without ever leaving it,
three of falling,

falling in the shadow of the three days,
three days of shadow,
days and days of shadows falling,
the falling days,
the shadow days ...
CALL THE HOSPITAL, JACOB!
... three shadows ...

JACOB: Oh lord, Ruth, just sit there. Don't fall!
I'm calling an ambulance.

RUTH: ... falling in threes, shadows of three, ever
three, ever shadows, shadows, shadows ...

The Operating Theatre

RUTH, JACOB, RAFEL, AMEK, ZABI: The
scene is an operating theatre.
I am on the table.

RUTH: I am waking ...

JACOB: ... waking ...

AMEK: ... waking ...

RUTH: I hear my heart beating, booming in my
ears.

ZABI: The operation complete.

AMEK: Anesthetic lapping thin.

JACOB: The room is wearing quiet.

AMEK: I can hear the sound of ruins of bricks crumbling to dust.

RAFEL: No, it is not that.

ZABI: I can hear the solid sounds of shoes on the floor.

RUTH, JACOB, RAFEL, AMEK, ZABI: And the breath of those hovering around me.

RUTH: No, it is my breath.

AMEK: No, it is the breath of the respirator.

RUTH: I thought I heard the sound of a choir of seventy angels, but it must have been my imagination wandering, wandering, wandering ...

RAFEL: That's it. Finishing up. Gauze wrap double weight. Take over, Doctor.

AS RUTH REGAINS CONSCIOUSNESS, SHE TOUCHES THE HEAVY BANDAGES ON HER MOUTH.

JACOB: It's all right. It's over now. Don't try to talk.

RAFEL: She's going to be fine. She's strong. You can go with her to recovery, but make sure she sleeps.

RUTH TRIES TO SAY "A CHOIR..."

JACOB: Shhh ... Doctor says you're gonna be fine, just fine.

RUTH TRIES TO SAY "THE TOWER..."
"

JACOB: Shhh ... Doctor says I can take you to recovery. You're gonna be all right. You're gonna live till you're a hundred and eight. But you're gonna need a lot of rest. Go to sleep ...

RUTH DROPS OFF TO SLEEP FOR AN INSTANT, AS IF MOVING THROUGH A PASSAGE. THE OTHERS FADE AWAY AND SHE RISES FROM THE TABLE REMOVING THE BANDAGES FROM HER MOUTH.

RUTH: Like refugees we lined up outside what had been our tower, now transformed into chambers of forgetting. A third of it had been sunken into the ground, a third had been burnt, and a third was left standing. Everyone who looked upon the ruins began to forget. There was a chamber for each person and after sleeping forty days and forty nights the slate was blank. There was no choice. To drive from our minds the sound of that onslaught we had to forget everything we knew. Most of us did forget and live in relative peace. Haunted by a feeling of dull remorse, but out of the path of that howling chaos.

But there are a few,
and I am one,
who never forgot.
I contained the memory,
wrapping the pain in layers, over and over,
so that it became
like a pearl.

RUTH PLACES A PEARL ON HER TONGUE. BESIDE HER, JACOB WRESTLES WITH AN ANGEL. LIGHTS FADE.

The End

LUSCIOUS MUSIC

Luscious Music: Preface to a Prelude

Luscious Music, as of the date of this publication, awaits its first production. I want to gratefully acknowledge the theatres and institutions that have supported it through its growth with readings, workshops, and publications: Dance Theatre Workshop, David White, Artistic Director, The Swiss Architecture Museum of Basel, Francesca Ferguson, Artistic Director; New Dramatists, Todd London, Artistic Director, Joel Ruark, Managing Director; Primary Stages, Casey Childs, Artistic Director, University of Alabama at Tuscaloosa Theatre Program, Paul Castagno, Chair; The Flea Theatre, Jim Simpson, Artistic Director, Carol Ostrow, Managing Director; The Labyrinth Theater summer intensive, Philip Seymour Hoffman and John Ortiz, Artistic Directors; Working Theatre, Robert Arcaro, Artistic Director; Cherry Lane Theatre, Angelina Fiordellisi, Artistic Director; Rattlestick Theatre, David Van Asselt, Artistic Director; New York Theatre Workshop, James Nicola, Artistic Director, and Ted Shank and Adele Edling Shank at *TheatreForum*. I also want to acknowledge with special gratitude Michael John Garcés who directed many of these incarnations.

CHARACTERS

CLEA SALCEDO CANTOS, sales agent for an automotive shop, Cuban-American, 30's

FRANK MCCAFFERTY, foreman for the shop, married to CLEA, late 30's

SONY SALCEDO CANTOS, office manager, CLEA's sister, 30's (note: Sony rhymes with Tony)

HARRY CHALMERS, electrician at the shop, lives with SONY, 30's

MITCHELL WILCOX, owner/operator of the Wilcox Autoworks, Viet Nam vet

TIME AND PLACE

The present. Winter in Southern Florida. A working class neighborhood of small tract houses off Route 27, between Miami and Orlando. CLEA and FRANK live next door to SONY and HARRY, down the road from the Wilcox AutoWorks.

ACT I

Scene

CLEA AND FRANK'S.

CLEA: So we're not going to talk about our little trip to court.

SONY: I'm not gonna bring it up.

CLEA: Tonight we're just going to slow down and have a nice game of poker and everyone's—

SONY: I wanna go somewhere.

CLEA: This is for Frank. He wants to play and get his mind off all this—you owe him.

SONY: Can I wear your leopard-skin visor?

CLEA: No, girl, that's for the pros.

SONY: I don't want you looking so sexy!

CLEA GRABS SONY IN A PLAYFUL TUSSLE. FRANK ENTERS. HELAUGHS AT THE ANTICS OF HIS WIFE AND SISTER-LAW.

CLEA: (pushing Sony off) He's here!

SONY: (to Frank) Is Harry bringing the rum?

FRANK: Your man don't know whether to rum*ble* or rum*ba*.

SONY: You! Stop teasing me or I'll do something to you that your wife won't like.

FRANK: Okay okay, he's bringin' the rum!

CLEA: Hey, Sony, help set up, and check under the chairs, 'cause our Frank here, he likes to stash extra cards.

FRANK FLOURISHES A DECK OF CARDS.

FRANK: Only when I'm doin' my show: The Amazin' Frank McCafferty, Maestro of the Divino Furioso Card Spectaculo!

SONY: Doesn't matter because I'm taking all your money tonight.

FRANK: (suddenly serious) You already did.

CLEA: Don't start on her.

SONY: Yeah, lighten up.

FRANK: Maybe now's a good time to get into it.

CLEA: We're supposed to be playing poker tonight.

FRANK: We can't keep bailin' your sister outa jail.

SONY: Don't mind me.

CLEA: What's this, *tough love*?

FRANK: No, we gotta get her some help.

SONY: I'm not really here.

CLEA: How to shoplift without getting caught?

FRANK: A shrink.

SONY: That's a laugh.

CLEA: Sony's already ate two social workers.

SONY: Three.

FRANK: Maybe it's time we put her some place.

CLEA: NO!

SONY: Those places are Thorazine hellholes.

CLEA: I promised my mother *on her deathbed* that I would take care of Sony. Do you know what that means?

FRANK: Clea! The cops keep catchin' her red-handed stuffin' shit in her pockets. It's like she wants to get caught.

CLEA: We always stay together. When the boat— That's the way it is with our family.

FRANK: What's one more Cubana in prison, huh?

CLEA: She just needs to get right with Harry— he's been threatening to leave her and that sets her off.

FRANK: What if Wilcox finds out—

SONY: Who's gonna tell him? Me? "Sorry, boss, I missed my shift, but I was in the slammer for stealin'."

FRANK: You're crazy enough.

CLEA: Don't use that word about my sister.

FRANK: I can hear him now: "You mean you put a thief in charge of my books?!"

SONY: You know damn well I'm never off a penny.

FRANK: I love you too. I'm just tryin' to figure this out. What about a shrink?

CLEA: "Tell me, my dear, did you ever have sexual feelings for your father?"

FRANK: They have drugs.

CLEA: Haven't you had enough trouble with that shit?

FRANK: That's low.

CLEA: I'm sorry. (no response) I'm sorry.

FRANK: Yeah, listen, I gotta get back to—

SONY: Frank! Give her a chance!

CLEA: You know that puttin' her on drugs isn't gonna cure what's wrong underneath!

FRANK: I haven't touched it in over fourteen months.

CLEA: You're not bein' fair.

FRANK: All right, Clea, forget it. What about Sony?

CLEA: Kiss me.

FRANK: We can't just keep driftin' along *hopin'* things are gonna get better.

CLEA: (teasing) Who *does* your hair?

FRANK: (deciding to play the role of the slickster) A good dye job's gettin' harder and harder to find. I had a gal in Nashville did my hair to a white light. I was always catchin' her outa the corner of my eye. Damn fool, went and married a cop.

CLEA: Shut up and kiss me.

FRANK: Look at those lips.

CLEA: Well?

FRANK: What a pucker.

CLEA: Come on.

SONY: Kiss her!

FRANK: How do you do that?

CLEA: Do what?

FRANK: Make 'em go like that.

CLEA: Family secret. You ever hear that song?
(singing)
> Let's make luscious music,
> No sounds so fine
> As your lips on mine...

FRANK: Mmmm, they smell like va...nil...la.

CLEA: You're supposed to kiss 'em, not smell 'em.

FRANK: I know what you're doin'.

CLEA: Betcha don't.

FRANK: You think 'cause I'm a prisoner of love
you can distract me with a flick of the lips.

CLEA: Does that make me a bad person?

FRANK: Maybe.

CLEA: Goddamnit, Frank, you better kiss me.

FRANK: And then we're gonna deal with it.

SONY: No!

CLEA: Yes!

FRANK: All right, but just one.

CLEA: We'll see.

THEY WRAP IN A KISS.

SONY: You find trips to the cops arousing, huh?

CLEA: What are we gonna do with you?

SONY: I gotta have things.

CLEA: You don't need men's cologne and baby wipes and—

SONY: I got it for Harry.

CLEA: Harry smells just fine without—

SONY: How d' you know how Harry smells, you don't—

CLEA: And you don't have a baby.

SONY: Maybe I'm gonna.

CLEA: You're too much. Frank, go tell Harry he's having a baby.

FRANK STARTS FOR THE DOOR.

SONY: Frank. Stay here?

FRANK: Jesus, Sony, it took five hundred bucks to bail you out this time.

SONY: You'll get it back.

CLEA: That's not the point. It's bad enough you get caught for the stealing you did, but why confess to three robberies you didn't do?!

SONY: How d' you know?

CLEA: Because you were on the road with me!!

FRANK: I'm gonna get Harry.

SONY: Don't tell him we're havin' a baby.

FRANK: I won't.

SONY: I'm not.

CLEA: Then why'd you say it?

SONY: We're not doin' too good. He told me I'm nuts and he's—

CLEA: You made mistakes, but that's gonna change. It's gotta. You heard the judge. One more conviction and it's three strikes, prison time.

FRANK: I'm gonna get Harry and get this game started.

FRANK LEAVES.

SONY: And what's so wrong with prison? At least you know where you are.

CLEA: They take away your rights.

SONY: What rights? In prison, you get three meals a day. At work, we get one break. In prison the biggest bastardo is called the warden. At work he's called Wilcox, and I—

CLEA: Stop playing.

SONY: What am I supposed to do?

CLEA: Go back to school.

SONY: Teach me how you keep things so good with Frank.

CLEA: We got couple simple rules when we fight, no name calling, no hitting. I swore when we were little, watching the way Papi hit Mami, I'd never let that happen.

SONY: Papi never hit—

CLEA: Don't start.

SONY: Frank never hit you?

CLEA: No.

SONY: You never hit him?

CLEA: Loca.

SONY: What about biting?

CLEA: (laughing) Biting—sure! (pause) You're gonna be okay. Harry's a good man. He works hard, he don't drink too much (not like Carlos), he wants to have kids.

SONY: Why's that so important? (no response) So do it.

CLEA: Stop torturing me. You know how bad I— Ya know, Frank's getting straight, and I'm traveling all the time and—

SONY: God, I hate it when you're gone!

CLEA: That's right, so when we can slow down enough—bang!

SONY: Bang! Oooh that feels good. Then we take the little one and Frank and Harry and show them Havana.

CLEA: Castro killed Havana.

SONY: That's propaganda.

CLEA: You know what his own wife said?

SONY: You know who he really loved?

CLEA: Yes, his wife, Mirta.

SONY: No he loved Celia.

CLEA: His *legal* wife Mirta said, "Ah poor Cuba. If he's as good a ruler as he was a father, [then poor Cuba.]"

SONY: (finishing CLEA's phrase in unison] "Poor Cuba." We can't talk about this.

CLEA: And you got a good man so cut him some slack.

SONY: Okay, okay.

CLEA: Okay?

SONY: Okay.

CLEA: Let's set up the table.

AS THEY PREPARE THE TABLE, FRANK AND HARRY COME IN. HARRY HOISTING A BOTTLE OF RUM.

FRANK: Look who I found.

SONY: (screaming) Harry!

HARRY SCOOPS UP SONY IN AN EMBRACE.

HARRY: I was lost and now I'm found!

SONY: I wanna win tonight, you gonna help me?

HARRY: Mi casa es su casa.

FRANK: It's every man for himself.

CLEA: What about women?

FRANK: What's the difference?

SONY: Com'ere, I'll show ya.

CLEA: Harry, grab her.

HARRY: Oh, I got her.

SONY: Let me check the deck.

FRANK: Yeah no cheatin' tonight, no decks with six kings.

SONY: Look who's talking.

FRANK: I never cheat—you never heard the McCafferty code?

HARRY: Yeah, never give a sucker an even break. Remember that time we took those truckers for—

FRANK: What I do is *bluff*—gonna bluff you touristas blind.

HARRY: Yeah, we'll see. Everyone, assume the position.

EVERYONE HUNKERS DOWN AT THE TABLE IN POKER MODE.

FRANK: Watch me now—who's dealin'?

CLEA: Me.

HARRY: Go girl.

CLEA: This game is five-card stud.

FRANK: If we're drawin' cards, it's called five-card *draw*.

CLEA: I don't care, I'm namin' it after you, *stud*.

SONY: I'm gonna get rich. Who's hidin' the rum?

HARRY: I *am* rich. Under your chair, sweet lips.

SONY: It's only temporary.

FRANK: Like everythang.

HARRY: Keep it light, Flash.

CLEA: Everybody ante?

SONY: Frank, put your money in.

CLEA: Okay, Harry, start the biddin'.

HARRY: I'm in for five.

SONY: Yeah.

CLEA: I'll do that. Frank?

FRANK: Green flag.

CLEA: Okay. How many?

HARRY: Take three.

SONY: Two.

FRANK: Two.

CLEA: And I'll take one.

PAUSE AS THEY CHECK THEIR HANDS.

CLEA: Harry, start?

HARRY: I'm stokin' the pot with ten.

SONY: I'll do your ten and raise you ten.

HARRY: Oooh, macho girl. What're ya gonna do, Clea?

CLEA: I'm staying in for the twenty.

FRANK: Stayin's my middle name.

HARRY: And I'll cover.

CLEA: Okay, whaddya got?

HARRY: Pair of KINGS!

FRANK: Red flag.

SONY: Read 'em and weep, pair of aces.

CLEA: Well, you got it. Pair of deuces.

SONY: Hot damn, I'm caliente! Come to mami!

HARRY: If we wanna get rich why don't we just grab the week's receipts—

FRANK: Wilcox says there's no cash flow.

SONY: Not true. You wanna know where it's really going? He's cooking the books.

CLEA: But can you prove it?

SONY: For every dollar we take in he puts a dollar in his secret account.

HARRY: Yeah and Sony's got the key—we dip in and rip it up to Chicago? Wilcox'd never catch us.

SONY: You're no thief. You'd get us caught for sure.

HARRY: Frank can drive the getaway car. It'll be wild.

SONY: Yeah! Running! I can see us now: shootin' it out with the heat on our tail, me and Harry chewing face between the ka-ching and the ka-peewww, maybe for the last time, 'cause I'm bleeding from a bullet grazed my forehead, my hair's flyin', fuckin' alive!

FRANK LEAPS UP AND RIDES HIS CHAIR LIKE A SURFBOARD.

HARRY: Will ya do it?

FRANK: I'll hydroplane all the way to Havana! Viva Fidel!

CLEA: You want to get our house bombed?! You put a lid on that commie shit, you Yanqui Dog!

FRANK: YEAH! I am the Yankee Dog! (grinding like Elvis the Pelvis) Bow wow, bow wow-*SITA*. You ever seen a dancin' dog put the pedal to the metal?!

CLEA: (laughing) You're a silly man but you're an excellent dog.

SONY: So we're gonna do it?

CLEA: Count me out.

SONY: Ahhh—why?!

FRANK GETS UP TO RELIEVE HIMSELF IN THE YARD.

CLEA: Where you goin'?

FRANK: Gonna see my parole officer out in the bushes.

SONY: Can I come?

CLEA: (to SONY) Get back here and play your hand.

FRANK: (on his way out) He warned me about consortin' with known Cubans.

CLEA: Is he okay at work?

HARRY: Yeah, the guy works like a banshee. He's practically an automotive faith healer. He does the laying on of hands and the car purrs like a five hundred dollar an hour hooker.

SONY: And how would you know?!

HARRY: Don't worry, Wilcox doesn't pay me enough. You know that cheapster broke down this mornin' and told Frank he was doin' a "pretty good job."

CLEA: That guy makes me want to leave this place so bad.

SONY: El cerdo! [the pig]

CLEA: Is he taking his breaks?

HARRY: Only 'cause we make him. Says every dollar he clocks is one buck closer to his Paradise Garage.

SONY: What are you two worried about?

HARRY: He told me everythin's cool with parole.

CLEA: It is. I'll play his hand.

SONY WANDERS NONCHALANTLY BEHIND HARRY.

SONY: Lemme see what you got.

HARRY: Here's what I got.

HARRY PULLS HER PLAYFULLY INTO HIS LAB AND NUZZLES HER NECK.

SONY: You need a shave!

HARRY: I thought you liked it rough.

SONY: Don't leave marks, didn't your daddy ever teach you?

HARRY: Leave my daddy outa this.

SONY: That's what I love about you—your sense of humor.

HARRY: I thought it was my (zapping her) electric touch.

SONY: (pummeling his chest) You're a monster, you know that?

HARRY: Frank, get back in here! I need help!

FRANK: (entering) That's what I get for hirin' a guy with no experience.

SONY: Oh, he's got experience. You should see him go.

HARRY: Don't give my secrets away.

FRANK: That's not why I *hired* him.

SONY: That's why *I* hired him.

HARRY: Maybe I should ask for a raise.

SONY: Just ask, baby.

CLEA: Hey! We're playing poker. Frank, get back in the game.

HARRY: Come on, man, these women are killin' me.

FRANK: Okay everybody, let's see what you got.

THEY LAY DOWN THEIR CARDS AND HARRY TRIUMPHANTLY REACHES FOR THE POT.

SONY: NO!

HARRY: Yeah, I told ya, flush beats a straight.

SONY: No way!

CLEA: Yeah, baby, give your man his money.

SONY: Frank, tell 'em!

FRANK: Sorry, lil' sister, *The Impossible* has struck agin. Give it up.

SONY: I was gonna give it up, but later.

HARRY: I like cash in hand, thank you very much.

SONY: Why don't we change the game?

HARRY: To what?

SONY: Strip poker.

CLEA: You had too much rum.

FRANK: (laughing) Yeah, I'll have to get my special deck.

SONY: No, come on, why does it always have to be so goddamn dull around —

CLEA: Don't talk like a puta.

SONY: Who's calling who a puta?!

FRANK: Come on, she's just havin' fun.

CLEA: No! I'm getting sick and tired of her attitude.

SONY: *You're* a puta!

HARRY: Chill.

CLEA: I'm sick of your crazy ass!

SONY: And I'm sick of your bitching at me all the time.

CLEA: Who bails you out? Tu es loca!

SONY: You stop calling me that or I'll rip your —

FRANK: Stop it, both of ya!

CLEA: My fucking locita sister needs to be taught some respect.

SONY: And who's gonna do it?

FRANK: Harry, grab her!

FRANK GRABS CLEA AND HARRY RESTRAINS SONY. THE WOMEN ERUPT.

CLEA: Eres una puta desgraciada! (You're a disgraceful whore)

SONY: Lo qué te pasa es qué tú no se la sabes mamar! (The thing with you is, you don't know how to suck him off)

CLEA: Cómo te atreves, sucia?! (How dare you, you filthy whore?)

SONY: Y qué, tú no singas?! (What, you don't fuck?!)

CLEA: Vete para el carajo, puta ascerosa! (Go to hell, you disgusting slut!)

HARRY: (shouting above the din) I'll take her home.

CLEA: You get out of my house! Get out of my house! You stain my house! GET OUT OF MY HOUSE!!

HARRY DRAGS SONY OUT. CLEA CALMS DOWN ENOUGH FOR FRANK TO RELEASE HER.

CLEA: You see?

FRANK: Yeah, you both got tempers.

CLEA: No, she's always been nuts, ever since she was a kid.

FRANK: She's all right.

CLEA: Why are you always sticking up for her?

FRANK: I'm not.

CLEA: If I say she's nuts, she's nuts, I oughta know.

FRANK: Fine. Yesterday you told me not to say she was nuts.

CLEA: I changed my mind. Is that a crime?

CROSSFADE TO SONY AND HARRY'S.

SONY: Why didn't you stick up for me?

HARRY: I did—I pulled ya outa there.

SONY: That's sticking up for me? You hear what she said to me?! I *stain* her house!

HARRY: Maybe she just wasn't in the mood to see your naked ass.

SONY: Maybe I wouldna lost.

HARRY: Maybe I woulda, you want that?

SONY: How dare the bitch tell me—

HARRY: Let it go.

SONY: She got no right to—

HARRY: Hey! We're home now.

SONY: She's uptight—poor Frank must be dying! You think he ever gets laid?! No wonder they got no kids!

HARRY: STOP IT!

SONY: Don't you yell at—

HARRY: This is home—stop it—PLEASE.

SONY: You sound like Carlos.

HARRY: Don't compare me with that motherfucker.

SONY: "Baby, I'm gonna get some beer, I'll be right back." 'Cept he never said he was going to New York to get it.

HARRY: That's it, I'm outa here.

SONY: Where you going?

HARRY: I'm leaving. Your trouble with the law I've been trying to deal with, but now you're tryin' to steal your own sister's peace of mind. Where my suitcase?

SONY: I'll fix your favorite. I got some pompano.

HARRY: Where is it?

SONY: How's lemon butter and garlic?

HARRY: Where'd you hide the goddamned suitcase?!

SONY: Harry, please don't leave me. I won't do it any more.

HARRY: You said that too many times.

SONY: Why don't you try to be a little bit understanding. I don't know why I steal. You could help me figure it out.

HARRY: What's to figure out? You want stuff.

SONY: No.

HARRY: No?

SONY: No.

HARRY: No?

SONY: No!

HARRY: Then *what*?

SONY: I wanna feel warm, it makes me feel warm.

HARRY: Get a heating pad.

SONY: You heartless shit, it's screaming for help.

HARRY: You read that in a magazine?

SONY: No.

HARRY: Why haven't you ever seen a shrink?

SONY: How can you trust them?

HARRY: You got a sister. Lean on her. That's what family's for.

SONY: Your mama left you in the back seat of a car.

HARRY: Exactly.

SONY: So stay! (HARRY starts for the door) I'll tell you something else you wanna hear. (He stops but does not turn to her) Remember we were talking last week? Late at night ...

HARRY: We're always talkin'.

SONY: You said it was time ... And you always wanted one? (HARRY turns to her) I changed my mind.

HARRY: Why?

SONY: Because I'm ready.

HARRY: 'Cause I'm leavin'?

SONY: Yeah.

HARRY: That's no reason to have a kid.

SONY: Yeah, you see I was holding out, trying to be sure, but when I was hiding the suitcase it hit me—what I was doing was proof you were the right man.

PAUSE.

HARRY: Do you really have pompano?

SONY: Don't leave me.

HARRY: (embracing her) I'm not.

SONY: That's not what you said.

HARRY: I don't know what you got, but I can't seem to find my way outa here. What is it?

SONY: Promise.

HARRY: I love you.

SONY: And I love you. I 'm gonna get better.

HARRY: I ain't your ex.

SONY: He was always talkin' 'bout *home*.

- 129 -

HARRY: Okay, hard word.

SONY: What if I don't get better?

HARRY: I'm willing to take the risk.

SONY: I stole a car last week. There was a brand new convertible, cherry red, sittin' there with the keys in the ignition. This wave hit me—do it! And the next thing I'm driving around the exit ramps on Twenty-seven. I didn't even know where to go.

HARRY: You just got to remember that next time and—

SONY: No, it's not right. I gotta leave before I hurt you.

HARRY: It's my choice. I can help.

SONY: When I feel your hand on my face like this I know you're the kindest man I'll ever know. But when you're not here I get confused. I'm lost. ... I'd never forgive myself.

HARRY: No, we're gonna do it.

SONY: I can't.

HARRY: I'm gonna.

SONY: You can't.

HARRY: (holding her until she melts) We're gonna.

SONY: If you could only hold me forever ...

HARRY: (studying her as she drifts) Where'd you go? (no response) What's so funny?

SONY: I remember my family's street, La Calle Segunda. There was a loose cobblestone outside our door. One night when I lost one of my little teeth, I sneaked out and buried it under that cobblestone.

HARRY: I used to get nickels for mine.

SONY: Papi said Tooth Angel would come and take it when I slept. I didn't want her to steal my tooth.

HARRY: It's not stealin'.

SONY: I wonder if it's still there?

HARRY: Sure.

SONY: I wanna go see.

HARRY: Baby, I love you but you can't go back to Cuba, there's nothin' there for you. They took your house. They'll lock you up.

SONY: I was so happy there. I knew where I lived. Mami and Papi let me go anywhere I wanted because I always knew how to get home. They called me their homing pigeon. But where did everyone go? (no response) Poor 'Rique under the water.

HARRY: That wasn't your fault—the boat broke up.

SONY: Mami and Papi gone ... everyone ...

HARRY: You were just a girl.

SONY: If I hadn't called to Rique to swim he—

HARRY: Shhh... Come here and gimme a hug. (She allows him to fold her into his arms) You know what makes a home?

SONY: I wanna go back.

HARRY: Kids, that's what makes it.

SONY: Maybe.

HARRY: You said we could start tryin'. How 'bout tonight? (She pulls away) Feels right.

SONY: I think I ... too much rum ...

HARRY: Nothin' wrong with a little high.

SONY: I want ... I want it to be just right.

HARRY: Baby don't mind no rum.

SONY: I had a different ...

HARRY: What?

SONY: Can you be a little ... patient?

HARRY: I have.

SONY: A little more?

HARRY: Okay.

SONY: You're pushing.

HARRY: Yeah, but you said—

SONY: I'm not ready—not quite.

HARRY: You are really screwin' me around, like some goddamned yo-yo, up and down and all around, what the fuck do you care? "He don't nothin'. He's just an asshole sit around wait forever, who gives a fuck?!" Well, I'm sick of it!

SONY: Please, that's not—where you going?!

HARRY: (storming out) I'm not your fuckin' toy.

Scene

WILCOX'S OFFICE. HARRY WALKS IN.

WILCOX: Chalmers, sorry to call ya in, ya lazy sack of shit.

HARRY: To what do I owe the honor on *my day off?*

WILCOX: Look, there might be a state auditor asking questions and your job is to be polite but stupid.

HARRY
About what?

WILCOX: It's just tax shit, fuckin' bureaucrats shakin' down honest businessmen. Where's Sony?

HARRY: Don't worry, I'll tell her.

WILCOX: Why isn't she here yet?

HARRY: I'm sure she's got her shift covered, right?

WILCOX: Don't you worry about lettin' a gorgeous woman like that outa your sight?

HARRY: Did you call me for lessons from Dr. Love?

WILCOX: You're tryin' to tell me you never wonder?

HARRY: When it's good at home, and you know it's good, there's no need. You want me to sell you some Spanish Fly?

WILCOX: Look, son, I was teachin' technique in the whorehouses of Saigon before you even learned to choke the chicken.

HARRY: If you're such a master of Eastern Love then why you runnin' a garage?

WILCOX: Men can't live on love alone. Now what're you gonna say to anyone snoopin' round?

HARRY: I'm gonna tell him, uh, gee, uh, gosh, uhhhh, all I know is my boss is the horny Buddha.

WILCOX: You tell him all you know is your boss got the Purple Heart. That'll be a sweet touch.

HARRY: You wanna show me your scar?

WILCOX: You really got Spanish Fly?

HARRY: Nah, I don't need it. Do you?

WILCOX: Hey! Who signs your check?

HARRY: You got one for me?

WILCOX: Monday.

HARRY: You said Friday.

WILCOX: Just remember, and don't forget to tell your little fox.

HARRY: Yeah and you don't forget Monday.

WILCOX: You're a good man, Harry. If you were on fire, I'd piss on ya.

HARRY: Yeah, and if you was on fire, I'd call ya the Burnin' Bush.

WILCOX: Hey, look, I don't mind allowing my employees a little banter, but I don't tolerate sacrilegious talk, ya hear?

HARRY: What're you talkin' about?

WILCOX: You don't be makin' fun of the Burnin' Bush.

HARRY: Exodus, chapter three, verse two: "The bush burned with fire and the fire was not consumed." You know why?

WILCOX: Okay, get outa here, you're wastin' my time. (as HARRY's leaving) Look, she could do a lot better'n you.

HARRY: Screw you, *Mister* Wilcox. We could all do better'n you.

WILCOX: Remember, zip the lips.

HARRY: (as he's leaving) Monday.

Scene

CLEA AND FRANK'S.

FRANK: (playfully) Get offa me, I'm fulla grease.

CLEA: If you're not ready to walk, they got your ass in a sling. You hear me, babe?

FRANK: Just two more years.

CLEA: Sure you don't want a beer? (no response) Seattle.

FRANK: Why's everybody movin' to frikkin' Seattle?

CLEA: I'm sick of this place.

FRANK: This about last night?

CLEA: No. Selling auto parts all over goddamn America is deadly. I swear every time I'm on the phone with some sleazoid—it doesn't matter what town he's in—it's the same guy. And the road trips! I drive all over the devil's garden scopin' out second-class garages and county tracks. It's *old*.

FRANK: I like bein' near Daytona. It's gonna be a goldmine for us when we got our own garage.

CLEA: Why don't we find another track up North?

FRANK: And move away from your sister?

CLEA: What's keeping you locked up in this track?

FRANK: Who you been talkin' to now?

CLEA: Are you still thinking about driving?

FRANK: No.

CLEA: Harry tells me you took a car out on the track.

FRANK: I needed to drive it to see if I fixed it.

CLEA: You race around a track at 180 mph, but it doesn't matter how fast you go, you're going in a circle, don't you see?

FRANK: There's freedom in that speed.

CLEA: It's not real.

FRANK: How would you know?

CLEA: I drive for a living!

FRANK: It's not the same.

CLEA: Who got three speeding tickets rushing home to you?

FRANK: Good racers avoid collisions. Statistics prove you're safer on the track than the highway.

CLEA: Racing's an addiction.

FRANK: Drivers got such hope. You're always just one win away from turnin' your life around.

CLEA: And what about the flip side? The deadly accident.

FRANK: I'm here, aren't I?

CLEA: Typical. Even when a driver dies the others think, "It's never gonna happen to me." And the wives are too scared to say, "It's me or the car, honey," because it's the wives who'd be gone. It's a goddamn death wish!

FRANK: Bullshit! Drivers realize the danger, but it's what they do. The stuff about macho death wish, that's outsiders' talk. Lookin' in the rearview mirror only slows you down.

CLEA: See! That need to always go faster—that's what drove you to coke.

FRANK: That was just a mistake like takin' a curve too fast.

CLEA: I can't believe you're saying this. Are you slipping on me?

FRANK: No! I just got perspective now—I don't have to deny everything I ever knew just for you.

CLEA: You know the fans come 'cause they think someone might *die* on that track.

FRANK: Come on! It's a sport!! They love speed. Look at the first Olympics—runners! Horse races, dogs, the Dominicans even race cockroaches. Don't mean they got a sick fascination with death!

CLEA: Everyone gets a right up close look at what scares 'em. And the winning driver is the one who can shut off his feelings. That's denial not a sport!

FRANK: If you hate it so much, how are we gonna start a business buildin' race cars?

CLEA: I'm a hundred percent behind the shop.

FRANK: And I'm fine now.

CLEA: But you know what happens when you drive.

FRANK: I wasn't driving. I was testing.

CLEA: Frank, I know when you're lying.

FRANK: Goddamnit, don't say that to me! What the hell is Harry doin' tellin' you shit like that?!

CLEA: He had no choice. I told him I'd get Sony to dump him if he didn't take care of you.

FRANK: Now you're stooping to blackmail!

CLEA: There's nothing wrong with asking family to pitch in.

FRANK: He's not family!

CLEA: You know he is.

FRANK: I knew you didn't trust me. How am I supposed to stay straight if my own wife is spying on me?

CLEA: Now don't go paranoid on me now or I'll know—

FRANK: Man, I thought I took all the blows I was gonna have to—

CLEA: Don't you think I've taken some blows? I lost my whole family coming here.

FRANK: Ancient history. I lost my mother too. And look at Harry: poor guy never even knew his father or mother, but he's workin' doubles to buy a house with Sony.

CLEA: Your mother didn't drown in front of your—

FRANK: Where they die doesn't matter, it's—

CLEA: Oh yes it does. What you think is wrong with Sony?

FRANK: It wasn't her fault.

CLEA: Try telling her that. But your problem isn't just in your head. You gotta remember the doctor said it's chemical; getting straight affects hormones and blood sugar. You're healing.

PAUSE.

FRANK: I want to.

CLEA: And you will. And Sony will ... Anyways ... I gotta go.

FRANK: I've been thinkin'. How 'bout a dance floor next to the pool?

CLEA: You're teasing me again.

FRANK: Two more years of socking it away and we're set.

CLEA: Just 'cause we run our own business doesn't mean we can afford swimming pools and ballrooms.

FRANK: We're even gonna have a heliport 'cause this ain't just any garage. I'll be workin' on top Nascars. Those Daytona racers spend hundreds of thousands. And I'm the best. We're gonna build that championship car.

CLEA: And we're gonna have a nursery?

FRANK: How many kids you want?

CLEA: Lots.

FRANK: Wanna start now?

CLEA: You big sexy man, I gotta go.

FRANK: Omaha's too far.

CLEA: Why don't you kiss me goodbye?

FRANK: (as in the Irish definition of foreplay) Okay: "Brace yourself, Bridget."

THEY KISS LONG AND HARD.

CLEA: I guess you still love me. I want you to do me a favor when I'm away. Take care of Sony.

FRANK: Clea—

CLEA: It's not that hard. Just keep an eye on her.

FRANK: Aww shit.

CLEA: She hasn't stolen anything in weeks.

FRANK: That's Harry's job.

CLEA: They're doing good, but she could drive him out in a second, she's done it before.

FRANK: What if I say no?

CLEA: No more kisses.

FRANK: (quickly) I'll do it.

CLEA: You should stiffen your spine.

FRANK: What exactly should I stiffen?

CLEA: And I love *you*—but I gotta go.

FRANK: Great.

CLEA: Don't pout. And besides, you've got my darling sister to keep you company.

THEY KISS AGAIN, THEN CLEA PICKS UP HER BAGS AND LEAVES. FRANK GRABS A CLIPBOARD AND STARTS FOR THE DOOR. HARRY CATCHES HIM.

HARRY: She gone?

FRANK: Yeah.

HARRY: You want me to cop some shit?

FRANK: No.

HARRY: Am I in the wrong house?

FRANK: I told ya, I'm clean.

HARRY: Man, she's gone for a week.

FRANK: Six days.

HARRY: Oh, you got it bad.

FRANK: Yeah, from my window, looks like you got it bad.

HARRY: Seein' they're sisters, we know what the other's got.

FRANK: Bullshit, they're nothin' alike.

HARRY: Let's have a party. Little marching powder, *leetle mambo*, maybe a drive over to the coast for some long-legged passion fruit.

FRANK: You don't need me.

HARRY: Well, actually ...

FRANK: How much?

HARRY: Wilcox hasn't paid me for that overtime. I do the son of a bitch the favor of coverin' for him, and he says cash flow's tight. We're doin' record business.

FRANK: How much?

HARRY: How 'bout a hundred?

FRANK: Seventy-five.

HARRY: Ace. I'll give it back to you when he pays me.

FRANK: Or you'll be fixin' cars in hell.

HARRY: Sure you don't wanna go?

SONY ENTERS WITH URGENCY.

SONY: What're you two doin'? Wilcox is having a shitfit!

HARRY: Mr. Taskmaster here is just sendin' me to Miami. Gotta go and pick up some new cutting tool.

SONY: I thought we were going to the movies tonight.

HARRY: Duty calls. Ain't that right, Mr. Frank? (FRANK only scowls) He's a hard man.

SONY: Oh.

HARRY: I'll make it up to you.

SONY: Uh huh.

HARRY: Tell Wilcox I'm comin' to drown him in the port-o-san.

SONY LEAVES.

FRANK: If you wanna go skankin' around that's your business, but leave me out of it, ya hear me?!

HARRY: Hey! Chill, boy!

FRANK: I'm supposed to be takin' care of her, not helpin' you give her the shaft. You do it again, I won't be quiet.

HARRY: You got any idea what I'm goin' through? Huh?

FRANK: I think so.

HARRY: I *don't* think so. Every time she's ten minutes late I'm afraid I'm gonna get a call from the precinct. It's shakin' my nerves. I need some space to clear my head so I can come back and deal. You don't have to make me out to be some fuckin' snake just 'cause I need some down time. You walk a day in my shoes and I'll guarantee you'll be splittin' at the seams. Think about that, Mr. Voice of Morality. Sometimes it ain't pretty what a man's gotta do to stick around. Thank you for the cash. I'll see ya tomorrow.

FRANK: Don't you say I don't know.

HARRY: That's what I don't get.

FRANK: You *know* where I been.

HARRY: Man, we were tight. But where's the wild man who saved my ass from those redneck welders?

FRANK: Yeah and if I didn't owe *you* I'd fuckin' crack your head.

HARRY: Well, you stay outa my business.

FRANK: Not talkin' 'bout your business, I'm talkin' 'bout you jammin' that shit up my nose and not respectin' what I gotta do.

HARRY: All right, I respect it.

FRANK: You ain't got the problem I do—

HARRY: I got no problem at all.

FRANK: You don't wake up in a cold sweat.

HARRY: No I don't. (pause) I'll respect that.

FRANK: Okay.

HARRY: I work for ya, we'll keep it at that.

FRANK: Goddamnit, you're so goddamn—I didn't say that!

HARRY: Okay, okay. (long pause) Hey, you heard this one?

FRANK: Hit me.

HARRY: A skeleton walks into a bar and asks for a beer and a mop.

FRANK: Yeah? And?

HARRY: That's it.

FRANK: That's it?

HARRY: (laughing) Think about it.

HARRY LEAVES. SONY COMES BACK IN.

SONY: Where's he going?

FRANK: Thought you went back to work? (no response) Didn't you say Wilcox was having a—

SONY: Did you really send him to Miami?

FRANK: He's doin' double shifts, ease up.

SONY: Frank ...

FRANK: You're shakin'. What happened?

SONY: I feel real bad.

FRANK: Did Harry do somethin' to you?

SONY: No.

FRANK: Sit over here and calm down.

THEY SIT TOGETHER. SONY DISSOLVES IN TEARS.

FRANK: It's okay, I'm here, it's okay ...

SONY: No.

FRANK: Tell me whatsa matter?

SONY: I'm fine now, gotta go.

FRANK: I'll go with you.

SONY: No, I'm fine.

FRANK: Listen, I gotta go, too. Wilcox forgot I *told* him I was sayin' goodbye to Clea. And now, since he's throwin' a fit, I gotta go feed his memory a knuckle sandwich.

SONY: That's a real hobby with you two, isn't it?

FRANK: What?

SONY: Making up shit you're gonna do to Wilcox.

FRANK: Yeah, it's cheaper than the alternative: murder.

SONY: Not funny. You know he keeps a 38 in his desk? He was playing Russian roulette.

FRANK: (laughing) He's showed every girl there. That's his favorite line, "you wanna see my gun?"

SONY: You shouldn't joke about it.

FRANK: He doesn't keep it any more loaded than that other thing he's got don't fire.

SONY: (laughing) Okay. But two cars, and don't be tailgating me.

FRANK: Then keep your tail at top speed.

SONY: With pleasure. (pause) You think I'm attractive? (pause) The way you're grinning ... So why doesn't Harry want me?

FRANK: He's head over heels for you.

SONY: That why you're with Clea?

FRANK: The reason why two people click isn't just looks.

SONY: Oh yeah, then why?

FRANK: When Clea and I first moved in, I was three months out and tryin' to get clean, but I kept slippin'. One night in a bar I drank too much tequila and started flirtin' with this ugly gal. Next thing I knew I heard the phone ringin', and I said to myself, come on, Clea, answer the goddamn phone. Then I heard this voice answer and it wasn't Clea's. I pried open a lid and saw I wasn't in my own bed. I rolled over and looked. It was the two-bagger from the bar. I staggered home. Clea been up all night, sittin' there in her bathrobe, eyes streamin'. I told her I'd made a bad mistake, drunk too much, and woke up with a real ugly woman. I thought she'd kill me, but instead she threw me in the shower, cooked me breakfast, and shoved me out the door for a job interview. It was this one. I said to myself, if this woman is big enough to forgive me, then I'm always gonna love her. Up to that moment I *thought* I loved her, but then, I *knew* it in my bones.

SONY: Why didn't she leave you?

FRANK: Maybe she figured I was sick. Or maybe she made a calculation.

SONY: Not Clea.

FRANK: Yeah, she'd put a lotta time into me and didn't wanna throw it away. Or maybe to prove she could survive any bullshit I put in our way. Your sister has a will of iron.

SONY: Maybe she just couldn't help herself.

FRANK: Sony, Harry told me that he wants to—

SONY: You ever think her and me might have similar body parts?

FRANK: Why you goin' there?

SONY: I'm not afraid to think out loud.

FRANK: Harry's a guy who comes home at the end of the day. That's what you want. Some guys don't. Harry comes home.

SONY: I'm never sure I'll get what I need.

FRANK: That why you steal?

SONY: I don't steal.

FRANK: They showed us the surveillance tapes.

SONY: If a mother's got a baby and no job and she takes a bottle of milk for her baby, is that stealing?

FRANK: Is it good with Harry? (she smiles) Then why isn't that enough?

SONY: Do you ever wonder if it would be good with me? Don't look away.

FRANK: No.

SONY: I read in a magazine how to tell when your lover is lying.

FRANK: Only one problem with that: I'm not your lover.

SONY: Maybe you wanna be.

FRANK: Why do you talk like this?

SONY: Why do you let me?

FRANK: Let's get you back to work.

SONY: I saw you looking at me last night.

FRANK: When?

SONY: When I dropped the melon.

FRANK: Man's gotta live.

SONY: Your eyes were doin' more than living.

FRANK: Please ... I can't help what my eyes do, you gotta give me a break, I'm sorry.

SONY: I don't want you to apologize. I'm just spinning 'cause I'm so unhappy that Harry isn't looking at me like—

FRANK: Here's what you do with Harry. You throw him in the tub, scrub him up, cook him some fish, and invite him to bed. That'll straighten him out. Let's go.

SONY: Frank?

FRANK: What?

SONY: Can we talk like this again?

FRANK: No.

SONY: It helps me.

FRANK: Why?

SONY: You got it together.

FRANK: No I don't, not yet.

SONY: You're the best at what you do, you're gonna build a winning car, you're the life of the party, you're the sexiest man in—

FRANK: No, shit happened, and I still don't know why, so how do I know it won't happen again?

SONY: Like what?

FRANK: I wanted to be a driver more than anything. Drivers were my gods. I kept anglin' for a sponsor, but I didn't get a driver has to see *all the angles*; ya gotta have eyes in the side of your head. I'd impress 'em by how nothin' mattered to me but drivin'. Wrong. I got a reputation for bein' *difficult*. Harry's the one's got it together.

SONY: I'm not ready for that.

FRANK: You're contradicting yourself.

SONY: Maybe. Don't you ever?

FRANK: Sure.

SONY: You're not mad at me?

FRANK: No.

SONY: You're so good.

FRANK: Forget it.

SONY: No, I meant, I bet you're good.

FRANK: GODDAMMIT! Now stop it! (pause) See, now look at what you made me do! You know I got a temper. I'm trying not to lose my temper! GODDAMMIT!

SONY: I know where Harry's going! And you know it too!

FRANK: Well …

SONY: And you're standing there telling me what I should do and you're lying the whole time.

FRANK: That's not what I was—

SONY: It's time to stop lying to me.

FRANK: (opening his arms to calm her) Come here.

SHE EMBRACES HIM. SHE TIGHTENS HER ARMS AROUND HIS NECK. TOO TIGHT. HE TRIES TO GENTLY MOVE AWAY. SHE PUSHES HIM AWAY.

SONY: It's time to stop lying.

Scene

FRANK IS FIXING HIS SCREEN DOOR. WILCOX ARRIVES.

WILCOX: Can't stop workin', huh?

FRANK: Got a problem with the door.

WILCOX: Won't let you in or won't let you out?

FRANK: Funny. What are you doin' here?

WILCOX: It's on my way.

FRANK: No it's not.

WILCOX: Listen … just bein' neighborly.

FRANK: That's real nice. Hold this.

HE MOTIONS TO THE EDGE OF THE DOOR. FRANK TIGHTENS A HINGE WITH A SCREWDRIVER.

WILCOX: You got a pro on the job now. Built my own house.

FRANK: Tap it tighter.

FRANK MOTIONS TO A WRENCH. WILCOX TAPS THE DOOR TIGHTER TO ITS HINGE AND SLIPS THE WRENCH IN HIS BACK POCKET TO FREE UP BOTH HANDS FOR ALIGNING.

WILCOX: Sony said you were savin' up.

FRANK: You're talkin' to Sony a lot, aren't ya?

WILCOX: Look … sweet girl.

FRANK: Show her your gun?

WILCOX: What're you savin' for?

FRANK: Buy my freedom.

WILCOX: It's overrated.

FRANK: Like it.

WILCOX: Here ya are—Sunday—kickin' back, workin' on the shack. Hey that's good idn't? kickin' back, workin' on the shack.

FRANK: Wilcox, you're the funniest guy you know.

WILCOX: How much you got?

FRANK: Why?

WILCOX: You owe me.

FRANK: For what!

WILCOX: For hirin' you.

FRANK: If you're tryin' to make me an offer, you're goin' about it the wrong way.

WILCOX: What makes you think I would want to—

FRANK: I got more output than two guys. I'm workin' three stalls practically by myself.

WILCOX: Listen, I think of you like the son I never had.

FRANK: (laughing) Oh yeah!

WILCOX: I'm serious.

FRANK: You told me you got a kid!

WILCOX: Yeah, but he's refusin' to serve, won't join up.

FRANK: What are you after?

WILCOX: Listen ... what'll it take to keep ya?

FRANK: I'm not goin' anywhere—yet.

WILCOX: I don't want you competin' with me.

FRANK: Ah hah! Now we're getting' down to it.

WILCOX: I'd like to beat the shit outa you for fuckin' up your life the way you did. Fine boy like you.

FRANK: You're not my daddy.

WILCOX: Listen, how 'bout I put you on time and a half?

FRANK: Big deal, you only got me on three quarter scale now.

WILCOX: That's 'cause of your probation.

FRANK: For over a year!

WILCOX: Listen … If I do this I want you to sign a contract.

FRANK: There's somethin' you'd do legal?

WILCOX: I'll give you the pay, but you gotta sign a contract says you won't compete with me if you leave.

FRANK: Free country.

WILCOX: Not for you.

FRANK: Money says I can do anything I want.

WILCOX: Not for two years and within a hundred miles of my shop.

FRANK: Trouble with you is, you got no faith with your customers. I went over Burke's car last week—fine-tooth comb. Your work order said, "Find somethin." But there was nothin' wrong. I gave him his money back.

WILCOX: You son of a bitch!

FRANK: Now he'll be back, and he'll tell his friends, and you'll get more business.

WILCOX: You fuckin' asshole! That's my money you stole right outa my pocket! I oughta have you locked—

FRANK: You're fuckin' nuts! Cost you nothing and earned you good will and—

WILCOX: Cost me the money I paid you! I didn't hire you to give my money away, you stupid motherfucker! Did I say you could decide who to charge?

FRANK: I was doin' the honorable thing!

WILCOX: You twisted fuck! That's why they locked you up in the first place! You got no values! You stole from me!

FRANK: Goddamnit, no I didn't!

WILCOX: That's my money! YOU GOT NO RIGHT!

WILCOX IS RIGHT UP IN FRANK'S FACE. FRANK PUTS HIS HAND ON WILCOX'S CHEST AND SHOVES HIM. WILCOX STAGGERS, LOSES HIS BALANCE, AND FALLS DOWN.

FRANK: Just leave me alone.

FRANK TURNS BACK TO HIS TASK WITH THE DOOR. WILCOX TAKES THE WRENCH OUT OF HIS BACK POCKET AND RUSHES AT FRANK, RAISING IT TO STRIKE. FRANK HEARS HIM COMING AND TURNS JUST IN TIME TO AVOID THE FULL BLOW, BUT IT GLANCES OFF THE SIDE OF HIS HEAD, STUNNING HIM.

FRANK: (groaning) What the …

WILCOX: I'm sorry, son.

WILCOX DROPS THE WRENCH AND LEAVES.
FRANK STAGGERS INTO THE HOUSE. TIMES
PASSES. HE'S HUNCHED IN A CHAIR
HOLDING HIS HEAD WHEN SONY ARRIVES.

SONY: He did this?!

FRANK: Go away.

SONY: I can't. Clea called and told me to take
care of you. I brought you a burger.

FRANK: Your sister has lousy timin'.

SONY: What happened?

FRANK: The son of a bitch—I told him I gave
Burke his deposit back. I just wanted to get his
stinkin' face outa mine. He landed flat on his
back.

SONY: You and your stubborn code of honor.

FRANK: I went back to work, and the fuckin'
jackal came up behind me and hit me in the head
with my own wrench.

SONY: Jesus, let me see.

FRANK: Owww!

SONY: Why aren't you dead?

FRANK: I heard him comin'.

SONY: (examining) Oh yeah ... I'm gonna clean this up. Where's the first aid?

FRANK: Medicine cabinet.

SONY: Okay, don't move. Eat.

SONY CALLING FROM THE BATHROOM.

SONY: Where is it?

FRANK: Try underneath.

SONY: Where?

FRANK: UNDER! DOWN BELOW! WAAAY DOWN!

SONY: Got it.

SHE'S BACK. SHE SETS TO WORK ON HIS HEAD.

SONY: You gotta stop fightin'. The year's only a couple months old and you've already had two.

FRANK: Those weren't fights.

SONY: Yeah? Why's your head bleedin'? From makin' love?

FRANK: My head doesn't bleed when I make love.

SONY: This is gonna sting.

FRANK: Oww!

SONY: Shhhh, shhhhh, Sony's gonna make it better.

FRANK: He can't fire me 'cause I'm the only guy who can prep a camshaft, hell, I'm the only one who can—

SONY: He won't have to fire you if he kills ya.

FRANK: Or if I kill him.

SONY: Qué macho. Can I feel your muscles?

FRANK: Sony!

SONY: Ah poor baby, c'mere, I'll make it better. (he shakes her off) No, come on, don't move, just lean your head back on me like that. That's it.

FRANK: Hmmm ...

SONY: You grunt nice.

FRANK: Hmmm ...

SONY: I learned this from a Malaysian laundry woman whose father was a healer. Agnes, real big gal, mounds of fat, but gifted. Just one finger movin' in circles around the center of your temples. She called it *The Touch*.

FRANK: It's good.

SONY: Yeah, let your shoulders go.

FRANK: My own wrench, he used my own—

SONY: Shhhhhh ... (pause) Listen to my fingers. What are my fingers sayin'?

FRANK: Hmmm ... I hear 'em.

SONY: You sure your head doesn't bleed when you make love?

FRANK: (trying not to laugh) Stop, don't make me laugh.

SONY: I think it does.

FRANK: It hurts when I laugh.

SONY: Yeah, I can see it now ...

FRANK: I don't. You could ask your sister.

SONY: I think I will.

FRANK: (in heaven) Ahhhhhhh, yeahhh ...

SONY: You starting to feel better?

FRANK: That's real nice. You got the touch.

SONY: That's what Big Agnes called it.

FRANK: Maybe you could move in here full time and do this.

SONY: I'd like that, but I don't know about Clea.

FRANK: But isn't that the definition of family?

SONY: What's that?

FRANK: When you knock on the door they gotta let you in?

SONY: So that's the way you feel about me?

SHE CUFFS THE BACK OF HIS HEAD.

FRANK: Owww!

SONY: Put your head back, damn, you're difficult! You give Clea this much trouble?

LONG PAUSE.

SONY: Hello? (no response) Where'd you go?

FRANK: (groaning) Uhhhh …

SONY: What—what's happening?

FRANK: Migraine.

SONY: Oh, Frank honey.

FRANK: Oh my fuckin' head hurts, I wanna scream.

SONY: Go ahead.

FRANK: (screams) AHHHHHHHH …

SONY: Okay.

FRANK: Where's Clea?

SONY: She's not here.

FRANK: What happens when you keep goin' down and there's just no bottom?

SONY: I'll catch you.

FRANK: MAKE IT STOP HURTING.

SONY: I know a way.

SONY KISSES FRANK ON THE MOUTH. HE PULLS AWAY.

SONY: What's wrong? (long pause) Don't you want it? (long pause) I do.

FRANK: You gotta get outa here. (long pause) Now.

SONY: Please.

LONG PAUSE.

FRANK: Before it's too late.

SONY WALKS OUT THE DOOR.

Scene

*NEXT MORNING. HARRY AND SONY KNOCK
ON THE SCREEN DOOR.*

FRANK: Go away!

HARRY: Frank, Wilcox wants to apologize.

FRANK: He what?

SONY: You heard him.

FRANK: (barking) Why you standin' out there?
(they start in) And shut the door! Damn
mosquitoes are bigger n' pelicans!

HARRY: Man, you are in one nasty mood.

FRANK: I'm bein' nice.

HARRY: He wanted to know where you were, so I
told him you were nursing "a cranial contusion."
He's pissin' himself you're gonna press charges.

FRANK: And sue that motherfucker for his whole
miniature cracker car shop.

HARRY: That too, so he told me to tell ya he'd
give ya two hundred bucks if you'd forget it.

FRANK: (laughing in spite of himself) Two hundred bucks!

HARRY: Yeah and he said it like you'd think it was a lotta money.

FRANK: Okay, here's what I'll settle for. I'll forget it for nothin' less than two hundred and *one* dollars, plus his left nut in a pickle jar. Sony, you go tell him.

SONY: Harry, why don't you?

FRANK: NO! Sony goes.

HARRY: What gives? I wanna see his face.

FRANK: I gotta talk to you about a thing.

SONY: You boys telling secrets?

HARRY: You okay?

FRANK: Yes, goddammit!

SONY: Clea said he'd be like this.

HARRY: Okay, Sony, you go, we gotta humor him.

SONY: I don't know what you got to talk about that I can't hear.

FRANK: It's just business.

SONY: Is it about me?

HARRY: Are you business?

SONY: I'm my business.

HARRY: Exactly. So no big.

SONY: 'Cause I don't talk about other people's business, I never do. Never. I never talk.

FRANK: Don't worry. Nobody's talkin' about nothin'.

HARRY: Now you're both bonkers. Sony, please help me here.

SONY: Harry?

HARRY: Son', I love ya, now hurry back with what our nutless wonder says.

SONY: Okay.

HARRY: Bye.

SONY: Bye, Frank.

FRANK: Bye.

SONY: Frank?

FRANK: What?

SONY: Bye.

FRANK: We trapped in a loop here? I said bye.

HARRY: Sony!

SONY: Okay.

SHE LEAVES.

HARRY: So what's all this about?

FRANK: Did you score?

HARRY: Yeah, you want?

FRANK: (hesitates) No!

HARRY: Then what's all this about?

FRANK: Fuck you.

HARRY: Hey man, I'll just wait till you get it all off your chest.

FRANK: What's goin' on with Sony?

HARRY: She just left. What's that got to do?

FRANK: Are you sure she's straight with you?

HARRY: She's cut the klepto act, but ... but if she'd just listen to me, we'd have a kid. That'll give us— I'll check on you later. I got a lotta work to do fillin' in while you're *playin' dead*.

FRANK: I'll go with ya.

HARRY: You got Sony comin' back!

FRANK: She knows where she lives. Right next door, right?

HARRY: Frankman, you are loopy. (raising his hand) How many fingers?

FRANK: (leaping up) Six! I feel fuckin' great! Let's go, I'm drivin'.

HARRY: I don't care if the pit boss said you were the most brilliant mechanic ever run a crew, I can't let you drive. Come on, maybe we can catch the poor woman before she—

FRANK: I'm tryin' to tell you somethin'!

HARRY: Okay, I give up. What?

FRANK: How well do you really know her?

HARRY: How well's any one ever know any one?

FRANK: Don't get all philosophical on me, Mr. One-Year-of-College.

HARRY: I know her better than anyone I ever met.

FRANK: Except maybe me.

HARRY: 'Cept you.

FRANK: You know why Wilcox was showin' her his phony Russian roulette trick? Maybe you gotta go deeper.

HARRY: You're startin' to piss me off.

FRANK: When I was livin' with Sheila one night I accused her of doin' all my coke. She threw —

HARRY: Sony's not gonna throw boilin' water on my back!

FRANK: She got me on assault. I figured with the burn I didn't need a lawyer, just take off my shirt. Little did I know her lawyer was the judge's nephew. A year in the state pen.

HARRY: Just 'cause we fight doesn't mean— I did my time.

FRANK: You never did time.

HARRY: Hell I didn't. They called it an orphanage, but I'll lay odds it was meaner than your state pen. Didn't I ever tell you about when I met the Devil?

FRANK: Mr. D.?

HARRY: The Prince *his-self*. I was cuttin' a lock on the window bars. Three in the mornin'. The nightman was passed out—his usual pint. All of a sudden I feel a tap on my shoulder. I whirl around and there's this thing with three heads.

FRANK: Shit!

HARRY: The head on the right looks like a mailman, the one in the middle looks like a painting, and the one on the left is a baboon but with human eyes. The mailman and the baboon are laughin'. The painted head gestures to look down, and when I do, I can see the puddle formin' round my shoes. And I knew who it was. (pause) I always wanted to come to Florida 'cause I love palm trees.

FRANK: You can't leave me hangin'! What the hell happened?!

HARRY: The nightman woke up. They put me in the cage for a month. (pause) Will you be my best man?

FRANK: How'd you get there?

HARRY: What's the problem?

FRANK: Well ... you're not actin' like you wanna get married.

HARRY: When I was on my way to Miami I saw a sign, *Wilcox AutoWorks*, with a palm tree painted on it. It was talkin' to me. And you *know* who was in the office. She gave me a smile that lit me up. When Wilcox hired me I knew it was that smile that did it, so I went back and asked her out. At the movie, for no reason, she leans over and pops a kiss right on my cheek—I fell in love.

FRANK: Is that enough?

HARRY: It's all there is.

FRANK: Okay. (pause) I'll do it.

HARRY: Great, but I'm still not lettin' you drive. Let's go before *I* hit you with a wrench.

FRANK: Just remember I know where you went last night.

HARRY: Oh I get it. This is the Evil Frank. Come on.

FRANK: I'm the Lizard King.

HARRY: Sure, and I'm your Siamese twin, let's go.

Scene

SONY AND HARRY'S. LATE THAT NIGHT.
SONY HAS FALLEN ASLEEP TRYING TO WAIT
UP. HARRY COMES IN, GUILTILY, ON CAT'S
FEET. SHE AWAKENS, GROGGY.

SONY: What time's it?

HARRY: Go back to sleep.

SONY: No deje el camino por coger la vereda.
("Don't stray from the path" from *De Camino a la Vereda* by Ibrahim Ferrer)

HARRY: You know I don't understand Cuban.

SONY: Com'ere and gimme a baby.

HARRY: I been workin'.

SONY: I want one.

HARRY: Not now — I stink.

SONY: Enrique can't swim.

HARRY: What?

SONY: (opening her arms to him) I'm ready.

HARRY: You take some pills?

SONY: I watched Wilcox today. He transferred half the week's receipts into his offshore account.

HARRY: That's none of my business. How many did ya take?

SONY: I don't never steal from *people*.

HARRY: He's not stealin' from people.

SONY: It scared me.

HARRY: You shouldn't take them pills.

SONY: Will ya hold me?

HARRY: It's hot.

SONY: Why won't you hold me?

HARRY: I told ya.

SONY: You been with another woman?

HARRY: Shut up.

SONY: Then com'ere and let me smell ya.

HARRY: Get away from me.

SONY: Harry!

HARRY: I'm takin' a drive.

HARRY LEAVES. SONY GOES NEXT DOOR AND FINDS FRANK IN BED, ASLEEP.

SONY: Frank?

FRANK: (startled awake) What're you doin'?

SONY: I couldn't sleep.

HE TURNS THE LIGHT ON AND FORCES HIMSELF TO FULL WAKEFULNESS.

FRANK: Why don't you go home to Harry?

SONY: We had a fight.

FRANK: Another one?

SONY: He's gonna leave me.

FRANK: Now did he say that, or you makin' it up?

SONY: Don't you think that I—

FRANK: Because you've been known to exaggerate.

SONY: No, he's gonna leave me, I can feel it.

FRANK: "Feel it" isn't evidence in court.

SONY: Are we in court?

FRANK: No.

SONY: Frank?

FRANK: Yeah?

SONY: Can I get in the bed with you?

FRANK: No.

SONY: I don't mean I wanna do anything, I just don't wanna be alone.

FRANK: No.

SONY: All right.

FRANK: Good night.

SONY: All right, I'm goin' to the store, you want anything?

FRANK: It's the middle of the night.

SONY: It's open all night.

FRANK: Don't go there.

SONY: You worried about me?

FRANK: No, it's just that—what would you need that can't wait?

SONY: They got a sale on cologne and baby wipes.

FRANK: You don't need those.

SONY: You and me know that.

FRANK: I'm supposed to be takin' ...

SONY: Then why don't you?

FRANK: I want you to go home to bed.

SONY: You worried I'll get caught?

FRANK: No—it's just late. You heard the judge, next time's three strikes and you do real time. And I've been there, you won't like it.

SONY: So you are worried.

FRANK: Do you know what it would do to Clea?

SONY: I won't get caught.

FRANK: No!

SONY: I got a new technique.

FRANK: NO!

SONY: Can I get in there with you?

FRANK: Sony. (long pause, she turns to leave)
All right.

SONY STARTS TO GET UNDRESSED.

FRANK: Leave your clothes on.

SONY: Fine, I'll leave the essentials on, but let me
get this bulky stuff off.

SHE UNDRESSES AND SLIPS INTO THE BED.

SONY: Frank?

FRANK: The answer is no.

SONY: How d' you know what I was gonna ask?

FRANK: Go to sleep.

SONY: Would you tell me a story?

FRANK: I don't know any.

SONY: Yes you do. (pause) I love your stories.

PAUSE.

FRANK: My father used to tell crazy stories when he was drunk.

SONY: Tell me.

FRANK: One night he told the same one over and over from midnight till dawn: There was an Irishman who lived in a shoe. When he grew old he went to sea as a ship's cook. He loved to cook shoes, old shoes. The sailors got sick of eatin' old shoes. They tied him to a rope and dragged him overboard until he became young again.

SONY: (laughing) That's wild. He told that all night?

FRANK: All night long.

SONY: (like a sultry blues) All night. (pause) Frank?

FRANK: What?

SONY: Would you kiss me goodnight? (he gives her a peck and turns away) Frank?

FRANK: What?

SONY: Would you kiss me goodnight again?

FRANK: There's been a monkey on my back.

SONY: I can get it off.

FRANK: No, this is the Monkey Demon. You put your hands on him and he bites them off.

SONY: Then just forget about him.

FRANK: He makes me think about you.

SONY: Then let's keep him.

FRANK: Why can't I stop thinkin' about you?

SONY: You want me?

FRANK: Won't I ever be able to stop makin' this move?

SONY: Shhh …

FRANK: Goin' straight and actually makin' it is hard to fathom.

SONY: Shhh … you don't know what you're talking about.

FRANK: Yes I do, this is the way down, I can feel it.

SONY: It'll be different this time.

FRANK: Do you know who I am?

SONY: Si.

FRANK: I mean, do you really know?

SONY: I really know. Wanna turn the light off?

FRANK: It's wrong.

SONY: None of that makes any sense when you need to get warm, when you're hungry, when you need to get loved. You've been set in your mind that you couldn't have me.

FRANK: Sony—

SONY: But you can. You just let go of all that's eatin' you. You let it all go. Into me.

FRANK: You make me feel like I'm drivin'.

SONY: It's simple.

FRANK: Real fast.

SONY: Yeah.

FRANK: Sony.

SONY: Just kiss me goodnight ...

ACT II

<u>Scene</u>

*CLEA AND FRANK'S. FRANK WALKS IN AND
FINDS WILCOX LOOKING AT SOME MAIL.*

FRANK: What the hell do you think you're doin'
in my house?

WILCOX: Look ...

FRANK: I could have you arrested for trespassin'.

WILCOX: Look now, I came to apologize, and I
brought you some compensation.

FRANK: Oh, yeah, *uh huh*, I see. You didn't want
anybody to see you doin' this, didja?

WILCOX: Look, here's the two hundred.

FRANK: Two hundred and *one*.

WILCOX: Yeah, sure, take it.

FRANK: I said two hundred and *ONE*.

WILCOX: Look, what're you crazy?

FRANK: It's not negotiable.

WILCOX: All right, all right.

WILCOX DIGS INTO HIS POCKET FOR THE
ADDITIONAL SINGLE AND FORKS IT OVER.

WILCOX: No hard feelin's?

FRANK: And I want the rest of the day off.

WILCOX: Look ... I need you to come in and —

FRANK: You need to see it my way or I'm gonna
sue your ass.

WILCOX: McCafferty, you got a screw loose.
Listen to me! How many other guys hire ex-coke
heads outa jail? Huh? You owe me!

FRANK: I don't care.

WILCOX: Look ... (long pause) Okay.

FRANK: It was a real pleasure seein' ya.

WILCOX: Okay, okay, sure. Take the day off. But the hoist is jammin'.

FRANK: You sound just like my old man, give me somethin' with one hand, take it away with the other.

WILCOX: The new kid got his foot caught, but just for a second.

FRANK: Goddamnit!

WILCOX: Don't worry, he's okay. I'll see you tomorrow.

WILCOX HEADS FOR THE DOOR. FRANK SHOUTS AFTER HIM.

FRANK: All right, I'll be there at three, and that's it!

WILCOX: (over his shoulder) And I can't give ya my left nut. Much as I know you been pining for it. 'Cause I'm gonna be needin' it.

Scene

CLEA AND FRANK'S. LATER THAT NIGHT.

CLEA: I'm gonna spit in his eye and quit.

FRANK: Not yet, we can't afford— He can't help himself.

CLEA: I can't figure you out. Half the time it sounds like you want to kill him, and then you turn around and it's like you love the guy.

FRANK: His temper hits boil and he's gone. We're the same.

CLEA: I been home eleven hours and all I get's a kiss, more like a peck. I was gone six days. Don't that make you think of doing something?

FRANK: I just wanna sit here.

CLEA: Rub my back?

FRANK: You never seen anyone just sit before?

CLEA: Why are you staring at the ceiling? (no response) You're scaring the shit outa me. (no response) I'll fix that Wilcox. I saw him pinching Dolores's ass. Can you imagine that poor woman, getting touched by the human hose. You ever see anyone sweat more than that man? All he has to do is sit and he drops a bucket on the floor. I'm gonna tell his old lady I saw him filling his fingers. That'll make him sweat.

FRANK: I don't want you to even talk to Wilcox.

CLEA: You're back! What's with this catatonic act? (no response) I had some of that as a kid. (no response) I'd lie in my bed with my arm in the air all night like this. My mother had a friend who had a sister who was a nurse, and she said the doctors in the hospital said that was a sign of catatonia.

FRANK: You slept with your arm in the air?

CLEA: Yeah.

FRANK: Which one?

CLEA: First one I put up.

FRANK: I knew there was a reason I married you.

SHE EMBRACES HIM HAPPILY. AT FIRST HE RETURNS HER KISS, BUT THEN PULLS AWAY.

CLEA: What's wrong?

FRANK: Nothing.

SONY ENTERS, SENSES THE TENSION, AND STOPS.

CLEA: You need something?

SONY: No.

SONY PROBES FRANK WITH HER EYES.

FRANK: What?

LONG PAUSE. CLEA LOOKS FROM FRANK TO SONY TO DISCERN WHAT'S GOING ON. FRANK GETS UP.

CLEA: Where're you going?

FRANK: Porch.

FRANK'S OUT THE DOOR. SONY STARTS AFTER HIM.

CLEA: Wait a minute. (pause) I owe you an apology.

SONY: For what?

CLEA: You remember.

SONY: No.

CLEA: For what I said when we had that ...

SONY: It's been two weeks.

CLEA: So you do.

SONY: That was ridiculous, "I stain your house."

CLEA: I know ... (pause) but you went too far.

SONY: This place is bad for me. I want to go home.

CLEA: We lived here twenty years. This is home.

SONY: No.

CLEA: You wanna go back to seven dollars a month rolling cigars?

SONY: Better than here.

CLEA: I can't help it Mami and Papi told us we were coming to dreamland.

SONY: And we're living with the wrong men!

CLEA: Speak for yourself.

SONY: Face it. Why don't you have a baby?

CLEA: You know why.

SONY: Can't your man give you one?

CLEA: Of course he can.

SONY: Then it's your fault. You lie there and shiver all frigid?

CLEA: The heat in my bed would burn you. You're talking foolish.

SONY: You're so foolish you don't even know how he really feels.

CLEA: You sound like some gutter slut, not the woman Mami and Papi raised us to be!

SONY: Don't even think about coming through my door. Stay out!

CLEA: Fine, don't come crawling to me!

SONY STORMS OUT. FRANK WALKS BACK IN.

FRANK: What she say to you?

CLEA: Her usual crap.

FRANK: What she *say*?

CLEA: That you're a son of a bitch.

FRANK: Why?

CLEA: She says she wants to go home. I could wring her neck.

FRANK: You're just pissed. Let her alone.

CLEA: Harry's a patient man.

FRANK: Maybe he's not the right guy for her.

CLEA: Who else would have her?

FRANK: Sony's so ... she could have any man she wanted.

CLEA: *Any* man?

FRANK: You know what I mean.

CLEA: If she's a saint, how come she tells her own sister not to come in her house?

FRANK: She didn't say that.

CLEA: Why are you always arguing with me about what she said? You know irritability's a symptom?

FRANK: You can't stop lookin' for signs, can you?

CLEA: I didn't mean it that way.

FRANK: Always doubting me.

CLEA: Not any more. (pause) Will you come to bed with me?

FRANK: Hmm.

CLEA: Come on.

FRANK: I'm gonna go check on the generator.

CLEA: It's late, can't you never stop working?

FRANK: If it's not runnin' in the mornin' we lose an hour.

HE STARTS OUT. CLEA LIFTS HIS KEYS OFF THE TABLE.

CLEA: Don't forget your keys.

FRANK: I'm gonna walk.

CLEA: You never walk to work.

FRANK: I need to burn off some—

CLEA: There's a beautiful moon, I'll go with you.

FRANK: No that's okay.

CLEA: We haven't taken a walk in—

FRANK: No, you need your rest.

CLEA: For what?

FRANK: Good night.

CLEA: Kiss me goodbye?

FRANK KISSES HER AND LEAVES. CLEA CAN'T SIT STILL AND WALKS TO THE DOOR. MOMENTS LATER, FRANK ENTERS SONY'S HOUSE.

SONY: I saw you coming. (FRANK is silent. Long pause) Harry said you sent him on another night job. (long pause) You wanna tell me about all his overtime?

FRANK: That's not why I'm here.

SONY: Did ya come for more?

FRANK: Yeah.

SONY: It was good, wasn't it?

FRANK: I haven't been able to believe it.

SONY: You wanna be sure?

FRANK: Yeah.

FRANK TAKES SONY IN HIS ARMS AND LIFTS HER ONTO THE TABLE. CLEA'S SILHOUETTE APPEARS IN THE DOORWAY. THEY DON'T SEE HER. SHE'S STARTLED BY WHAT SHE SEES, BUT SILENTLY MOVES AWAY.

Scene

CLEA AND FRANK'S, SLIGHTLY LATER. CLEA IS AT THE TABLE, A BOTTLE OF WHISKEY IN FRONT OF HER, UNTOUCHED. WILCOX KNOCKS AT THE DOOR.

CLEA: (screams) WHAT?

WILCOX ENTERS AND FINDS A DISTURBED CLEA.

WILCOX: Are you okay?

CLEA: What do you want?

WILCOX: I need to talk to Sony.

CLEA: (shouting) She lives next door! Go knock on *her* door!

WILCOX: I did, no one's home. Look, what's wrong?

CLEA: (exploding) What makes you think anything's wrong?

WILCOX: You and Frank have a fight?

CLEA: Mind your own business.

WILCOX: Look, maybe I can help, you know that next trip, why don't we call it off? I can get the specs from a guy I know—

CLEA: I hate this godforsaken place!

WILCOX: Look, Clea, I never had anyone as good as you, I been thinkin' that it was time I gave you a raise, to maybe—

CLEA: I don't want a raise!

WILCOX: You don't?

CLEA: I don't want anything!

WILCOX: How much that stuff you drink?

CLEA: Not a drop. Nothing makes any sense.
Nothing makes any sense! Nothing makes any
sense!

WILCOX: Well ... I'm gonna shove off. Listen ...
you gonna see her?

CLEA: NO!

WILCOX: Okay. (pause) Whatever it is, I'm
sorry. (pause) I like you. You're a good person, I
always—

CLEA: I am not a *good* person!

WILCOX: Okay.

CLEA: What are you doing here?!

WILCOX: Okay.

CLEA: What?!

WILCOX: Okay. (pause) Good night.

Scene

SONY'S. LATER.

FRANK: I gotta get back.

SONY: One more.

FRANK: No.

SONY: Why?

FRANK: I can't do this.

SONY: You *are* doing it.

FRANK: It's crazy.

SONY: It's what happened, that's all, it's not crazy. Not everything has to be judged.

FRANK: What if Clea finds out?

SONY: I'll never tell her.

FRANK: Shit has a way of comin' out.

SONY: It won't.

FRANK: It's impossible. You got a man, we live next door, we work together, we—

SONY: That's all true, just don't say—

FRANK: I can't.

SONY: Goddamnit, Frank! Something clicked, you can't deny that. Things happen for a reason.

FRANK: And what reason could this be?

SONY: I don't know.

FRANK: Maybe 'cause you're so fucked up?

SONY: You're more fucked up than I am!

FRANK: Yeah? Who conned her way into my bed?

SONY: Don't blame me for wanting you.

FRANK: You didn't want me, you needed me.

SONY: What the hell's the difference?

FRANK: Listen, Sony, I just can't do it.

SONY: That's not fair. I got no one to hold on to.

FRANK: You got me and Clea and Harry.

SONY: You and me both know where Harry is, and you heard my loving sister screaming at me to get out of her house.

FRANK: That was just a fight.

SONY: So is this.

FRANK: No it's not. There's a chance to get out 'cause it never really happened.

SONY: I'll handle this anyway you want. Fine— we don't tell anyone—once a week, once a month—fine, I don't care—just don't cut me off.

FRANK: I'm not cuttin' you off.

SONY: You bastard, yes you are!

FRANK: I'm not.

SONY: I'll be all alone.

FRANK: You live with all of us.

SONY: I live with nobody.

FRANK: Then nobody can help you.

SONY: Frank!

FRANK WALKS OUT.

Scene

NEXT MORNING. CLEA AT THE TABLE DRINKING COFFEE. FRANK POURS HIMSELF A CUP.

CLEA: Morning.

FRANK: Yeah.

CLEA: Sleep okay?

FRANK: Except for my head throbbin' like a jackhammer.

CLEA: Ouch. (pause) Hungry?

FRANK: Dunno.

CLEA: Want me to fix you something?

FRANK: Nah.

CLEA: Ya gonna work all day on coffee?

FRANK: No.

CLEA: Frank?

FRANK: Why d'ya do that, both you and your sister, why d' ya say, *Frank*? I'm right here.

CLEA: I can see that. And I'm right here, too. CAN YOU SEE THAT?!

FRANK: Hey! Whoa! What?!

CLEA: Okay, let's start again. (pause) Wilcox says he wants me to go to Little Rock next week.

FRANK: You just got back from a trip.

CLEA: He says we gotta increase our sales by twenty-five percent, or we can't make the nut.

FRANK: That's bullshit, we're doin' better than ever. Forget it.

CLEA: It's my job.

FRANK: I don't want you to go.

CLEA: Why not?

FRANK: What d'ya mean, why not?

CLEA: Why don't you want me to go?

PAUSE.

FRANK: (taking her hand) Listen, I've been— how 'bout if you and me go to the drive-in tonight, huh?

CLEA: You mean it?

FRANK: Yeah.

CLEA: And we'll park in the back?

FRANK: Guaranteed.

CLEA: I'll be there.

FRANK: Good.

CLEA: Frank?

FRANK: Why do you do that?

CLEA: I don't know.

FRANK: I'm lookin' right at ya.

CLEA: Okay. (pause) Frank?

FRANK: Yeah?

CLEA: I still have to go to Little Rock.

FRANK: NO!

CLEA: Why is it such a big deal all of a sudden? Somethin' wrong?

FRANK: Yeah. With Wilcox.

CLEA: Something wrong with you?

FRANK: No, I'm gonna go set him straight. What the hell does he think you are, a goddamned teamster? I'll see you later.

CLEA HAS STARTED TO CRY. BEFORE FRANK GETS TO THE DOOR HE NOTICES.

FRANK: What're you cryin' about?

CLEA: I don't know.

FRANK: I do somethin'?

CLEA: You shouldn't go until you ate some breakfast.

FRANK: I don't want any. What're you cryin' about?

CLEA: You should eat.

FRANK: I don't have time to cook it.

CLEA: I'll fix you anything you want.

FRANK: This is crazy. Stop cryin'! ... All right—fine!

CLEA: What do you want?

FRANK: I'll have eggs.

CLEA: Aghhh.

FRANK: We don't have any, do we?

CLEA: I'll go get some.

FRANK: No! Now cut this shit out! What the hell's goin' on?!

CLEA: You tell me! I walk in this house and it's like I'm living with a pod man. Well, I'm gonna snap you out of it. You sit there and you wait for the eggs I'm gonna cook you, and you like 'em, or I'm gonna divorce you, you hear me?!

FRANK: Yeah.

CLEA: I'll be right back.

Scene

SONY AND HARRY'S. LATE. SONY'S SITTING ALONE WITH A BOTTLE. WILCOX KNOCKS.

SONY: Yeah?

WILCOX: It's me.

SONY: Who?

WILCOX: It's me.

SONY: What the ... (going to the door) Wilcox, what're you doing?

WILCOX: Can I come in?

SONY OPENS THE SCREEN DOOR. WILCOX COMES IN HOLDING A BOX OF CHOCOLATES.

SONY: Harry's not here.

WILCOX: I didn't come— I came to see you.

SONY: If he knew you were here he wouldn't be too happy.

WILCOX: Look, I uh, brought you this.

HE HANDS HER THE BOX OF CHOCOLATES.

SONY: Did you spend too much time in the sun?

WILCOX: They're real good.

SONY: You already eat one?

WILCOX: No.

SONY: Well thanks. You want to sit down?

WILCOX: Yeah.

SONY: You want a drink?

WILCOX: Maybe just wet my whistle.

SONY: Why do you think men bring women chocolate?

WILCOX: Look ... things aren't too good at my house.

SONY: Maybe you'd like to tell Harry when he gets home. He'll be home soon.

WILCOX: I been sleepin' on the couch.

SONY: You look like it.

WILCOX: Look, I like you, I really like you.

SONY: You are a surprising man, Mr. Wilcox.

WILCOX: Mitchell.

SONY: Okay. (pause) Do you want another shot?

WILCOX: Just one more, thanks.

SHE POURS HIM THE SHOT, WATCHES HIM DOWN IT, AND LAUGHS.

SONY: You got some on your chin.

WILCOX: I like the way you laugh.

SONY: Uh huh.

WILCOX: I like the way you tease Dolores.

SONY: She's a good person.

WILCOX: Look ...

LONG PAUSE.

SONY: What's the matter?

WILCOX: Would you move in with me?

SONY: I don't know what you're talking about.

WILCOX: I know I'm not a young man, but I wouldn't ask for much. We'd have money, and you'd have a lot of time off. I ain't never seen anyone as beautiful as you.

SONY: It's time for you to leave.

WILCOX: Now look, I don't mean you any disrespect.

SONY: I want you to leave now.

WILCOX: Why?

SONY: You don't have any right to talk to me this way.

WILCOX: It's not like I never did anything before showed you how I feel.

SONY: You never did nothing for me.

WILCOX: Look, I did you a lot of favors.

SONY: Yeah, name one.

WILCOX: I know all about your trouble with the law.

SONY: You what?!

WILCOX: Sheriff tipped me off. Listen to me, I never said anything about it. And it's on account of how strong I feel—

SONY: You shut up. I don't like this. This is not right.

WILCOX: I just want some kinda consideration here.

SONY: There's the door. Consider that!

WILCOX: Look—I gave you a break!

SONY: Now leave!

WILCOX: You're takin' a risk.

SONY: I'm trying not to lose it. Now go on!

WILCOX: Wait till you start gettin' old.

SONY: I know all about it.

WILCOX: You don't know nothin' about it. Sometimes when I catch a glimpse of myself in a mirror I get startled, like "who the fuck is that old codger?"

SONY: It doesn't matter for men.

WILCOX: That's why I want you, you make me feel young.

SONY: You're asking for trouble—wouldn't you always be suspicious of young guys?

WILCOX: I don't care. Just thinking of you I get hard.

SONY: You're talking shit, never gonna happen.

WILCOX: My old lady already sees me as old. She's ready to retire my ass in every way.

SONY: How do you think I see you?

WILCOX: As a man who can still get things done. You know that.

SONY: I want skin that ripples.

WILCOX: If you and me was together I'd get back in shape.

SONY: Hormones aren't there.

WILCOX: Don't say that.

SONY: You're not *getting* old, you already *are* old.

WILCOX: You fuckin' bitch.

SONY: The thought of fucking you disgusts me.

WILCOX: There's one advantage of bein' old. You learn a thousand ways to hurt someone and, baby, you're on my list.

SONY: Your gums are puffy and white, and your teeth look like they're shrinking.

WILCOX: What if I was to lose my temper and do somethin' I'd regret, like call the cops and tell 'em you were stealin'? Can't we compromise here?

SONY GOES TO THE DOOR AND HOLDS IT OPEN, HER FACE RED WITH CONTROLLED RAGE.

SONY: Good night, Mr. Wilcox.

Scene

SONY AND HARRY'S. NEXT MORNING. HARRY, HALF-ASLEEP, AT THE TABLE. SONY ENTERS.

SONY: Get home late?

HARRY: You were passed out on the—

SONY: That's not what I asked.

HARRY: Leave me alone, I'm not even awake.

SONY: What time you get home?

HARRY: I tried to wake you but you musta taken too many sleepin' pills *again*.

SONY: Don't try 'n turn this around.

HARRY: You gobble up a buncha pills, pass out, and then freak when you don't know—

SONY: You're not taking care a business.

HARRY: What's that mean?

SONY: It means if you were smart you'd keep the back door locked.

HARRY: Are you threatenin' me?

SONY: You leave a woman alone enough they get—

HARRY: That's it! I'm outa here!

SONY: Good! 'Cause there's guys lined up.

HARRY: You're so fulla shit!

SONY: You have no idea.

HARRY: Ten minutes with you'd send any guy runnin'.

SONY: Some guys can go longer than ten minutes.

HARRY: Okay, I'll call your bluff.

SONY: A lot longer.

HARRY: Who you got?

SONY: None of your business!

HARRY: You got no one! And you're never gonna have no one 'cause you're a liar!

SONY: You're lying to me right now!

HARRY: You screwed me over. You got me waitin' around for a promise you got no intention—

SONY: I made you no promise that I—

HARRY: You told me we were gonna have a kid and—

SONY: That was no lie!

HARRY: And every time it was time it was time to wait!

SONY: That's not true, what about the time when—

HARRY: Don't gimme your connivin' shit, I'm sick of bein' strung along like I was some fool— like I was—

SONY: You don't even listen to me when—

HARRY: 'Cause you're a twisted liar and that's why you're never gonna have no one.

SONY: Oh yeah! I got someone.

HARRY: It sure as hell ain't me!

SONY: That's right!

HARRY: You're gonna fuckin' die ALONE!

SONY: I got some—

HARRY: No one! You got no one!

SONY: Get out now!

HARRY: NO ONE!

SONY: I got Frank!

THEY BOTH FREEZE.

HARRY: What the fuck're you talkin' about?

SONY: That's right. I'm giving Frank a taste. He's very grateful.

HARRY: You're lyin'.

SONY: That man goes for hours. He can go hard. Then he coasts. And he glides. And then he does this percussive thing sends me places can't be found on a map.

HARRY: I'm gonna kill him.

HARRY RUNS NEXT DOOR. FRANK IS STILL SITTING AT THE TABLE AS HARRY BURSTS IN.

FRANK: What the—

HARRY: You're fuckin' Sony!

FRANK: Did she tell you that?

HARRY: Is it true?!

FRANK: It was a mistake.

HARRY: You're fuckin' right about that!

FRANK: It's over. Lemme ex—

HARRY: YOU MOTHERFUCKER!

*HARRY LUNGES AT FRANK'S THROAT. A
BRAWL, THE MEN ROLLING AND PUNCHING.
HARRY IS ON TOP OF FRANK TRYING TO
STRANGLE HIM WHEN CLEA WALKS IN WITH
A BAG OF GROCERIES. SHE DROPS IT AND
RUNS AT HARRY, KNOCKING HIM OFF FRANK.*

CLEA: STOP IT! STOP IT! STOP IT!

*HARRY AND FRANK PULL THEMSELVES TO
THEIR FEET, HEAVILY WINDED.*

CLEA: What in hell are you doing?!

HARRY: He's fuckin' Sony.

*CLEA SLAPS HARRY'S FACE AND WALKS OUT.
THE MEN STARE AT EACH OTHER, SPENT.*

*CLEA SLAMS OPEN SONY'S DOOR TO FIND
HER SITTING AT THE TABLE WITH TWO
EMPTY BOTTLES OF SLEEPING PILLS. AS SOON
AS SHE HEARS THE DOOR, SONY MAKES AN*

AWKWARD ATTEMPT TO COVER THE BOTTLES.

CLEA: Goddamn you!

SONY: Mami?

CLEA ATTACKS, REPEATEDLY CUFFING SONY.

CLEA: What did you do?! What did you do!

SONY: Stop! Please stop!

CLEA: You have your own man! You puta!

SONY: Stop!

CLEA: Puta! Puta sucia!

SONY FALLS OUT OF THE CHAIR AND THE BOTTLES ROLL AWAY. CLEA SEES THEM.

CLEA: What are those?!

SONY: Nada.

CLEA: (picking up a bottle) What is this?

SONY: Nada.

CLEA: Did you take all of these?

SONY: I love you.

CLEA: Dios mio!

SONY: Inez is here, and Rique, and—

CLEA: Were the bottles full?

SONY: —and Ramon, he's so handsome, and Cecilia, how I've missed pequenita Cecilia, mi niña—

CLEA: Answer me! Did you take all these pills?

SONY: No, Rique, don't!

CLEA: Please, God, help me.

SONY: No, Rique! Don't try to swim, I didn't mean it! Go back!

CLEA: You stay awake. Stand up!

SONY: Rique! Go back! Rique!

CLEA: If you can't stand up— ! (as she runs out) I'll be right back!

CLEA FINDS THE TWO MEN STILL SITTING, STUNNED.

CLEA: Sony took a whole bottle of pills, maybe two, we gotta get her to the hospital! Come on, Frank, MOVE!

HARRY RUNNING FOR THE DOOR,

HARRY: Never mind him, come on!

CLEA: Frank!

FRANK CAN'T MOVE. CLEA RUNS OUT.

Scene

TWO NIGHTS LATER. HARRY IS EDGING OUT CLEA'S DOOR.

CLEA: Can't you stay for a while?

HARRY: I don't wanna run into him.

CLEA: No chance of that, he hasn't been home before dawn for—

HARRY: Still I don't wanna talk to the guy.

CLEA: But you must have to talk to him at work.

HARRY: He has Carcone relay everything. Can't even look at me.

CLEA: I need your help. He's spending all our money.

HARRY: On what?

CLEA: You know what. I want you to talk to whoever's dealing and tell 'em to cut him off.

HARRY: You know it don't work like that.

CLEA: Last night he got in another bar fight. Cop said he hit a guy over two hundred and eighty pounds.

HARRY: You might think I'm way off base for sayin' this, but you gotta cut him loose before he kills you both.

CLEA: Maybe giving everything's what you gotta do for love.

HARRY: You ever try to save a drownin' person? They try to climb up on top of you to get to the air. First thing you gotta do is immobilize 'em or they'll take you under with 'em.

CLEA: You and me are close. (no response) You mighta married my sister. (no response) She's asking for you.

HARRY: She remembers me — amazin'.

CLEA: She loves you.

HARRY: People vote with their feet.

CLEA: Why don't you move back in?

HARRY: Motel 6 suits me fine, nice pool, the ice machine's —

CLEA: She's coming home tomorrow.

HARRY: What! That's too soon!

CLEA: "Señorita, you got insurance? No? Too bad you tried to kill yourself, you're outa here in two days. Adios." She'll be all alone over there.

HARRY: Why don't you ask Frank?

CLEA: (pause) What's happened to you?

HARRY: What's happened to me?! Woman! Get it together! Start screamin' and trashin' shit and slappin' *him* upside the head! Burn the fuckin'' mattress! What the hell's wrong with you?!

CLEA: I'm doing all that! I could leave him, I could dump her, but then what do I got? Huh?

HARRY: I gotta go.

BEFORE HE CAN GET OUT THE DOOR,

CLEA: The doctor said she's probably pregnant.

HARRY: Oh fuck!

CLEA: They were gonna give her some drugs, psychotropics. (Sounds like an island.) So they asked if she might be pregnant. They gave her a blood test. They're not sure, but 'cause of this one hormone level it's likely. It could hurt the baby, so she decided no drugs. And she's freaking out about Wilcox.

HARRY: What makes you—

CLEA: She's scared he'll pin his skimming on her, and she won't even take a sedative. What'll we do?

HARRY: What makes you think I'm the father?

CLEA: Don't talk like that! It was only twice.

HARRY: That's one more than it—

CLEA: Then take a blood test.

HARRY: No way. (pause) You tell Frank about this?

CLEA: Well ... not ...

HARRY: You didn't tell him?

CLEA: (pause) Not yet.

HARRY: It's all too ... fuck ... I mean ... what the ...

CLEA: Please, Harry, I need you.

HARRY: All right ... I'll think about it, but I gotta go.

Scene

THE NEXT MORNING. SONY'S HOUSE. CLEA HELPS SONY IN THE DOOR.

SONY: Let me go, I'm fine.

CLEA: Good.

SONY: Where's Harry?

CLEA: At work.

SONY: You know what I mean.

CLEA: He's not comin' home.

SONY: Where?

CLEA: He's at a motel. (pause) Sit down and rest.

SONY: They made me lie in bed for two days. Where's Frank?

CLEA: At home. (pause) With *me*!

SONY: Subtle.

CLEA: I told Wilcox you were in the hospital with food poisoning. He expects you in tonight. Can you do that? (SONY nods) Now I'm gonna be checking on you on a—

SONY: No one asked you—

CLEA: Shut up, I'm doing it.

SONY: Hey, didn't you hear the doctor, don't upset me?

CLEA: I cleaned out your medicine cabinet and threw out all the pills, and I searched the house and—

SONY: You what?!

CLEA: You're gonna be here alone some, can you handle that?

SONY: You stay outa my shit.

CLEA: Okay, I'm not gonna upset you. (pause) Not in your condition.

SONY: (pause) Thanks for bringing me home.

CLEA: De nada.

SONY: Clea?

CLEA: Yeah.

SONY: You know ... I'm sorry about ...

CLEA: We're not gonna talk about that now.

SONY: Well when?

CLEA: I dunno—not now.

FRANK OPENS THE DOOR AND STANDS IN THE DOORWAY LOOKING AT SONY. LONG PAUSE WHILE FRANK AND SONY STARE AT ONE ANOTHER.

FRANK: Are you all right?

CLEA: Get out of here!

CLEA FOLLOWS FRANK HOME. WHISKEY HAS TRIGGERED A MANIC HIGH IN HIM.

CLEA: Where's the bottle?

FRANK: Why don't you go down to the store and buy yourself a *live* husband?

CLEA: How many times do I have to tell you—

FRANK: Get one with two brains in case one don't work!

CLEA: I don't blame you.

FRANK: I wanna find myself a train.

CLEA: You need some coffee or I need to find the bottle.

FRANK: My grandfather walked in front of a train. Other men on the track crew claimed he didn't hear it comin', he went back for a shovel. Who doesn't hear a train?

CLEA: You're not gonna get a chance to kill yourself, because if you don't shut up I'm gonna do it for you. Let's have a drink.

FRANK: I think I'd *plant* my feet and *lean* right into it, head first. That's gotta be a fast way to go, a speedin' freight head on. The power of it! Imagine ... all flowin' into you. I figure you'd see a sharp flash of light, then, zippo, gone. Peace.

CLEA: At least we could drink *together*.

FRANK: Not all together.

CLEA: It's not your fault.

FRANK: Yeah, you asked me to take care of her and ole Frank sure did a bang up job.

CLEA: It's as much my fault as it is yours.

FRANK: Whoop de do and jubilee and walla walla bing bang!

CLEA: I shoulda seen it coming. Now where's the bottle?

FRANK: Gone. Make sure you get one with five fingers—no I mean ten—and all ten toes. That sounds funny doesn't it? *Tentoes! Tentoes! Tentoes! Tentoes! Tentoes! Tentoes!*

CLEA: I don't want one! Yes, you screwed up, and, yes, you're a son of a bitch! But my sister was outa control. She's powerful, and you got trapped tryin' to hold on.

FRANK: She coulda died in there.

CLEA: She's alive.

FRANK: And Harry's hiney, hiney hine ...

CLEA: What?

FRANK: Gone.

CLEA: He's not.

FRANK: Not what? Not Harry?

CLEA: He woulda quit except Wilcox won't pay him, so he's sticking around till he gets his check.

FRANK: There's a gentleman.

CLEA: Don't go badmouthing him.

FRANK: I love Harry.

CLEA: And what if he does leave? She's in no shape to wait for. (pause) Why do these things ... God does strange things.

FRANK: Don't gimme that god shit! If there is a god, he's a bigger loser 'n me.

CLEA: Tu eres un pedazo de basura, that's for sure, but I'm gonna do what my papi used to— before Castro broke his back.

FRANK: Had *nothin'* to do with Castro—you people are—

CLEA: *You people!* (no response) He'd go around with a cart, and he'd pick up junk, and he'd turn it into things people wanted. He called himself the

Saint of Junk, 'cause he could see something shining inside of anything.

FRANK: Please, go away.

CLEA: That's what I'm gonna do. I'm gonna pick you up.

FRANK: Please ...

CLEA: 'Cause I know what's inside.

CLEA SITS NEXT TO FRANK AND LIFTS HIS GLASS TO INSPECT IT IN THE LIGHT. SHE RUNS HER FINGER OVER THE TABLE, PICKING UP SOME PARTICLES OF DUST, AND FLICKS THEM INTO HIS GLASS. SHE WATCHES THEM FLOAT TO THE BOTTOM, SEDIMENTS OF DESIRE.

CLEA: You ever watch particles float to the bottom of a glass?

FRANK: Plenty.

CLEA: Remind you of anything?

FRANK: No reason to ruin good liquor.

CLEA: I watched Sony's first marriage go sour, then she met Harry, and I watched that go. I vowed that wouldn't happen to us, so I developed my love insurance in case we started slipping. I can dye my body blue, or skydive into the bed, I got a thousand. Which one you want first?

FRANK: What?

CLEA: Were you listening to me? (no response. CLEA shouts) You can't treat me like this! Who pulled you outa detox? Twice! And who got you this job? And who found this house and used all her savings for the down payment? And who—

FRANK: I know all that and you're right.

CLEA: Then talk to me!

FRANK: I want to stop talkin'.

CLEA: Why? (no response) Why?

FRANK: Because nothin' I say is finally true.

CLEA: Okay, fine, but at least touch me, you won't touch me! (no response) I'm right here.

FRANK: I know.

CLEA: You can touch me.

FRANK: But I can't.

CLEA: This was my fault! I shoulda done something about Sony a long time before this happened. You even warned me.

FRANK: You think you did this?!

CLEA: Stop fighting me.

FRANK: I sold myself out long 'fore you got to me.

CLEA: Stop it.

FRANK: I'm trapped, and I did it to myself.

CLEA: Maybe I haven't said this before—I figured you understood—but I'll say it. (pause) I forgive you.

FRANK: I can't let you. I can't stand livin' a lie. I can't pretend everythin' is back to normal.

CLEA: I want it back.

FRANK: It's never gonna be back.

CLEA: Why not?

FRANK: Look what I did.

CLEA: She's home now.

FRANK: No.

CLEA: Why can't you accept what I'm giving you?!

FRANK: I don't want to do this, but you just don't get it.

CLEA: Stop.

FRANK: I want a divorce.

CLEA: NO! I love you!

FRANK: I don't love you.

CLEA: How can you say that?

FRANK: Not any more.

CLEA: I know when you're lying.

FRANK: I wanna kill myself.

CLEA: No more lies.

FRANK: I'm gonna kill myself.

CLEA: Don't talk like that.

LONG PAUSE.

CLEA: There's a right time to have this conversation and it's not now. I have to go to work.

FRANK: You don't work at night so—

CLEA: We'll talk later.

CLEA LEAVES. FRANK POURS ANOTHER DRINK. SONY SLIPS IN SILENTLY. SHE WATCHES FRANK.

SONY: Frank?

FRANK: Get outa here.

SONY: I wanted to see if you was all right? Are you?

LONG PAUSE. NO RESPONSE. SONY MOVES TO FRANK AND TOUCHES HIS SHOULDERS.

SONY: You want *the touch*?

FRANK: You scared me half to death! You know what that is on my head—you tryin' to kill yourself?

SONY: I'm sorry!

FRANK: And just waitin' for you to finish it off.

SONY: I don't wanna be alone over there.

FRANK: Ohhh no, Clea's comin' back, and—

SONY: No she's not. She went to work my shift for me. She won't be back till late. (pause) Feel better?

FRANK: Yeah, you're the blessed balm.

SONY: What's blessed balm?

FRANK: (with a savage edge) What my goddamn old man called whiskey.

SONY: So I make you drunk?

FRANK: (laughing in spite of himself) Yeah.

SONY: What was wrong with your old man?

FRANK: He's the one taught me how to work on engines. 'If it warn't for bad luck I'd have no luck at all'—that was me. Till I got out and met Clea.

SONY: And then I ...

FRANK: Yeah.

SONY: We fucked up.

FRANK: Truer words ...

SONY: We can make it better.

FRANK: NO! Don't touch me!

SONY: What's wrong with you? (pause) It won't happen again.

FRANK: How do I know you won't be over here the next time she leaves town? What makes you think I got any control over what I do? And you sure as hell don't have any.

SONY: Do you want it?

FRANK: Of course I want it.

SONY: Do you love me? (no response) Don't tell me you ... (FRANK slowly shakes his head) I can live with that. (no response) We gotta make her know it'll never happen again.

FRANK: You gotta convince me you're not gonna kill yourself.

SONY: I wanted to die then, but no more.

FRANK: You been fucked up a long time, what's different now?

SONY: I got a reason to live.

FRANK: What's that?

SONY: The baby.

FRANK: What baby?!

SONY: I'm gonna have a baby, didn't Clea tell you?

FRANK: No!

SONY: Why not?

FRANK: How the fuck do I know why not?!

SONY: Well I am.

FRANK: Whose is it? (no response) Oh God!

SONY: I don't care.

FRANK: Oh no ...

SONY: I was putting Harry off, so maybe ...

FRANK: Shut up!

SONY: It might be you and me.

PAUSE.

FRANK: You know how bad Clea wants one?

SONY: Yeah. (pause) But I'm gonna love this baby no matter 'cause I'll finally have someone who's gonna love me.

FRANK: So you're not gonna try to do it again?

SONY: Will you hold me? (pause) Just for a little?

FRANK EMBRACES HER. THEY CLING TO ONE ANOTHER. CLEA ENTERS, SEES THEM AND APPLAUDS. THEY LEAP OUT OF EACH OTHER'S ARMS.

CLEA: Qué lindo.

SONY: What are you doing here?!

CLEA: I live here.

SONY: You're supposed to be working my shift.

CLEA: I've been sitting in the car, timing you.

SONY: No, you don't understand!

CLEA: I wanted to see how long it'd take you to shake your culo over here. Impressive.

SONY: It's not what it looks—Frank, explain her what—

CLEA: Frank, I couldn't admit this before, but you're lost. There's nothing I can do about it, and if I stay I'll go under with you.

SONY: No! Don't say—

CLEA: (to SONY) Get out!

SONY: No, you don't get it!

CLEA: Yes, I do! How many times I gotta throw you outa my house?! GET OUT!

SONY: Frank, I'm sorry.

SONY LEAVES. FRANK MOVES TO CLEA AND TRIES TO TAKE HER IN HIS ARMS.

FRANK: Clea ...

CLEA: What are you doing? Are you crazy?

FRANK: Listen to me.

CLEA: Get away—

FRANK: Please?

CLEA: NO!

LONG PAUSE.

FRANK: You never said no.

CLEA: You're on some death trip and I got too much life, I don't wanna ... I don't wanna do it ...

FRANK: I'm gonna try.

CLEA: I don't care.

FRANK: I think she's gonna be okay.

CLEA: I don't care.

FRANK: Please, you got it wrong.

CLEA: Shut up! I always believed love is total sacrifice. When you go that far some miracle happens. You hear me? (no response) Frank!

FRANK: What?

CLEA: Where is my miracle?!

FRANK OPENS HIS ARMS TO HER. SHE SLOWLY SHAKES HER HEAD. SHE PULLS OUT A SUITCASE AND BEGINS TO PACK AGGRESSIVELY. FRANK WATCHES HER A LONG TIME.

FRANK: I love you.

CLEA: I know when you're lying.

FRANK: I'm not.

CLEA: You're so bad at it.

FRANK: Bullshit. When we sat right here and had breakfast you had no idea I fucked your sister the night before.

CLEA: You're wrong, I saw it through the door.

FRANK: Liar!

CLEA: You had her on top of the table.

FRANK IS STUNNED FOR A MOMENT, MORTIFIED.

FRANK: And you didn't say a word! You let me sit here and make a fool of myself. That's worse than a lie!

CLEA: You're worse than a lie!

FRANK HITS HER. CLEA RECOVERS. A LONG
PAUSE WHILE THEY STARE AT EACH OTHER.
DEVASTATED BY WHAT HE'S DONE HE SINKS
TO HIS KNEES. FINALLY, CLEA WALKS TO THE
SUITCASE AND PICKS IT UP.

FRANK: I'm so sorry.

CLEA: I know.

FRANK: I'm so ...

AS CLEA STARTS FOR THE DOOR, HARRY
BURSTS IN.

HARRY: Clea!

FRANK: What're you doin' here?

HARRY: What're *you* doin' here?

CLEA: What's wrong?

HARRY: Wilcox is gonna bust Sony, he's gonna—

CLEA: Slow down—wait a minute! WHAT?!

HARRY: I was leanin' on Wilcox for my check. He said the company's missin' a lotta money, and Sony's why.

CLEA: What the—

HARRY: He said she was stealin', and he's gonna call the cops.

CLEA: That bastard's gonna try to pin his embezzling on her!

FRANK: That ain't gonna happen.

HARRY: What could you possibly do 'bout it? (no response) Right.

CLEA: Frank, what's the name of that lawyer?

FRANK IS LOCKED INSIDE A FATAL CALCULATION. THEY STARE AT HIM.

HARRY: HEY!

FRANK: I'm workin' somethin' through.

FRANK MAKES A REALIZATION AND A DECISION. HE STARTS FOR THE DOOR.

HARRY: Great! Sony's in trouble and you're walkin' out?

CLEA: Frank! They'll lock you up again, what good'll that do Sony?!

FRANK: If you're not ready to walk, they got your ass in a sling, didn't you say?

CLEA: Let us handle—

FRANK: Why don't you kiss me goodbye?

CLEA: Stop!

FRANK: Your sister's gonna be okay.

FRANK LEAVES.

HARRY: What a fuckin' waste that guy is, I can't believe—

CLEA: Maybe you should go. I don't wanna fight about—

HARRY: No, I'll shut up, we got work to do.

CLEA: All right, I'll hit the yellow pages for lawyers. You go talk to Dolores and Juanita.

HARRY: You think they'll go along?

CLEA: He owes them back pay too, right?

HARRY: Wilcox is gonna lean on 'em. So let's get 'em on tape before the pressure hits. I'll go get a tape recorder.

CLEA: Yeah, then bring 'em over as soon as they get a break.

HARRY: (on the run) Gone.

Scene

WILCOX'S OFFICE. FRANK LOADS WILCOX'S GUN AND RETURNS IT TO THE DESK DRAWER. THEN HE SEARCHES THE DESK FOR WILCOX'S COOKED BOOKS. HE FINDS THE LEDGER. AS WILCOX RETURNS, FRANK PUTS IT BEHIND HIS BACK.

WILCOX: What the fuck's wrong with you?! There's no Feds out there!

FRANK: Just a test. The way you flew out that door seems you got a guilty conscience. You're gonna blame it on Sony?

WILCOX: That bitch is bankuptin' me.

FRANK: She never stole a penny from you.

WILCOX: I'm dockin' you for this shit! Now get out!

FRANK: (revealing the ledger) You won't be dockin' no one from a jail cell.

WILCOX: That's none of your fuckin' business! Gimme that!

FRANK: Make me.

WILCOX: She's a thief and you know it.

FRANK: I saw the way you looked at her.

WILCOX: Give me the goddamn book, I'm warnin' ya! Don't make me lose my temper!

FRANK: Did you hear the one about the con who dropped his dentures?

WILCOX PULLS THE 38 OUT OF HIS DRAWER AND POINTS IT AT FRANK.

WILCOX: Last chance.

FRANK: I know you've been cookin' the books.

WILCOX: You'll never prove it!

FRANK: And I'm callin' the cops.

WILCOX: Oh you wanna be dead!

FRANK: You and I both know the gun ain't loaded.

WILCOX: There's always one bullet in Russian roulette.

FRANK: You didn't even take off the trigger guard.

WILCOX: (releases the trigger guard) I used to think you were smart. Why you doin' this?

FRANK: Go ahead and cock it.

WILCOX: Maybe you're gettin' some of that sweet stuff, is that it?

FRANK: That's good, big man, now pull the trigger.

WILCOX: Where do you want it?

FRANK: (pointing at his heart) What're my odds?

WILCOX: One in six. You ready?

FRANK: Yeah.

WILCOX: You son of a bitch.

FRANK: What's the matter? You comin' up short?

WILCOX: Now you're really pissin' me off!
You're a helluva poker player. But this is it!

FRANK: Now I'm gonna dial the phone.

FRANK LIFTS THE RECEIVER.

WILCOX: GODDAMNIT! Don't push me!
HANG UP!

Scene

*CLEA AND FRANK'S. HARRY HAS GIVEN CLEA
THE FATAL NEWS. SHE'S WAILING.*

CLEA: No! please, no ... no ... no ... no ... no
... no ...

HARRY: (embracing her) I know ... I know ...

CLEA: Frank, why'd you do this to me?

HARRY: I'm sorry.

*CLEA EVENTUALLY RECOVERS ENOUGH TO
PULL AWAY.*

CLEA: How do you know what ... happened?

HARRY: He got Dolores and Juanita to listen.

CLEA: He's always got a plan.

HARRY: Kept baitin' him, "Go ahead and cock it— Now I'm gonna dial the phone." Then they heard the shot.

CLEA: Oh Jesus ... he made him do it.

HARRY: When the cops took Wilcox away, he was screamin' he never loaded the gun.

CLEA: May he burn in hell!

HARRY: Couldn't stop screaming, "It wasn't loaded!"

CLEA: What am I gonna do? I was walkin' out.

HARRY: (handing her an envelope) Dolores gave me this from him.

CLEA: Oh no, I can't.

SHE OPENS THE ENVELOPE AND PULLS OUT A RECEIPT.

CLEA: It's a receipt for a box of bullets.

HARRY: Damn, *he* loaded the gun.

CLEA: "Love always, Frank."

CLEA EXPLODES, TEARING HER HAIR,
TRASHING THE ROOM.

CLEA: How could he do that! How could he do
that! How could he do that! How could he do that!

HARRY WRESTLES WITH HER SO SHE WON'T
HURT HERSELF.

HARRY: Hey! Hey! Come on, I know, I know ...
(as she's slowing down) He saved Sony.

CLEA: I know that! (pause) But how could he do
it?!

HARRY: He found a way out.

CLEA: I love him so much.

HARRY: Yeah. (pause) A stubborn man.

CLEA: Goddamn him! Now look what he's done!
When Wilcox goes on trial for murder, I got the
evidence says it wasn't his fault!

HARRY: What're you talkin'?

CLEA: You think I want that on my conscience?! Goddamn you, Frank!

HARRY: You gotta be crazy!

CLEA: They could even put him to death!

HARRY: What d'you care what happens to him?

CLEA: I'd be helping to kill him.

HARRY: He's a murderer, for Christ's sakes!

CLEA: Frank made this happen!

HARRY: He was gonna frame Sony and —

CLEA: (torn and abruptly reversing herself) He shot my Frank!

LONG PAUSE.

CLEA: I'm leaving.

HARRY: No, don't do that.

CLEA: What's holding me here?

HARRY: Well ... the trial.

CLEA: I could come back if I ...

HARRY: And what about ... Sony?

CLEA: I'll bring her up there with me.

HARRY: I don't know if that's ...

CLEA: What are you trying to say?

HARRY: It wouldn't be good for her to move right now.

CLEA: There's no one to take care of her here.

HARRY: Well ...

CLEA: You?!

HARRY: I could.

CLEA: Do you love her?

HARRY: What's Sony gonna do when she finds out?

CLEA: Do you love her? (no response) Never mind, forget it, I gotta be alone now.

HARRY: Clea.

CLEA: Go on, go.

HARRY: All right goddamnit! (pause) Yes!

CLEA: I don't know what happened here. I ...

*SONY ENTERS AND FREEZES WHEN SHE SEES
HARRY. CLEA KISSES HIM ON THE CHEEK
AND HE STARTS TO LEAVE. SONY STEPS IN
FRONT OF HIM. A BEAT. HE EMBRACES HER
AND QUICKLY LEAVES.*

SONY: Did you see that? (no response) What's
the matter?

CLEA: You just get up?

SONY: Why you so upset?

CLEA: The usual.

PAUSE.

SONY: Did you see that?

CLEA: I'm busy now.

SONY: What does that mean? He didn't even say
anything!

CLEA: I know. I'm doin' somethin' now. Go home, and I'll be over in a little while to talk.

SONY: I love him so bad.

CLEA: I know.

SONY: I'll be quiet.

CLEA EMBRACES SONY AND WON'T LET GO.

SONY: Let me go.

CLEA: Shhh …

SONY: What's wrong?

CLEA: Nothing.

SONY TRIES TO DISENGAGE. CLEA HOLDS HER MORE TIGHTLY. SONY SURRENDERS. LIGHTS FADE.

The End

THE DESERT

The Desert: Preface

I wrote *The Desert* for Christina Lind and Heather
Lind. From fall 2006 to spring 2007 we met at
intervals, and I would share with them my pages,
sometimes as few as ten. Their response as they
inhabited their roles, and their feedback, impacted
the direction of the writing. In May of 2007 a
workshop was co-produced by Creation
Production Company and Here Arts Center,
Kristin Marting, Artistic Director. Lisa Paulsen,
the Director of Emory University's Playwriting
Center, afforded further development. When *The
Desert* receives its first full production it will be
because of the special contribution of Christina
and Heather, and I am very grateful to them.

CHARACTERS

KATRINE and MARIAN BOELKE, sisters

TIME AND PLACE

The present. Las Vegas. KATRINE and MARIAN work as croupiers at The Venetian. MARIAN works in the Baccarat Salon. KATRINE deals Blackjack.

My mother knew how hurtful a broken illusion could be.
Vladimir Nabokov in *Speak Memory*

When an unclean spirit comes out of someone it roams through arid regions searching for rest and does not find it. Luke 11:24

ACT I

KATRINE: You look good in widow's black.

MARIAN: Don't pretend to be insincere. Where is he now?

KATRINE: Too subtle for you?

MARIAN: It's time to be concrete.

KATRINE: You always have been.

MARIAN: I'm afraid you're mistaken.

KATRINE: Mother always was.

MARIAN: Concrete or mistaken?

KATRINE: She was never mistaken. (pause) I'm sorry for your loss.

MARIAN: At least I finally know where he is. Stop trying to change the subject. Where's Miguel?

KATRINE: Ask the army.

MARIAN: (pinning her like a laser) Where.

KATRINE: You're relentless! He's gone seven months and suddenly you demand to know where he is? How much are you willing to pay?

MARIAN: How do I know I'd get the truth?

KATRINE: Kick the tires.

MARIAN: Five hundred dollars.

KATRINE: Deal!

MARIAN: Well?

KATRINE: The truth is … I don't know.

MARIAN: He hasn't told you?

KATRINE: It's against regulations.

MARIAN: You think I'm paying you five hundred for *that*?

KATRINE: You didn't have it anyway. You're flat broke.

MARIAN: (insinuating that KATRINE's does not) My trust fund still trusts *me*.

KATRINE: I know we work in the most elegant casino in Vegas and your credit cards get denied.

MARIAN: You of all people shouldn't call The Venetian elegant. A cheap imitation of Venice— complete with gondolas.

KATRINE: (laughing) In the desert.

MARIAN: You drove him out.

KATRINE: Why's that always your theory?

MARIAN: With your insecurities.

KATRINE: You don't have to worry about me, honey.

MARIAN: I love your tough girl act.

KATRINE: What else can I do when they leave?

MARIAN: I was left, too.

KATRINE: Makes me want to get a gun.

MARIAN: No.

KATRINE: Why not?

MARIAN: Because you're my sister. (pause) How do we get past this?

KATRINE: Easier said than done.

MARIAN: No. First … we just *say* it: "We're going on." I've got a plan for us to start over. Listen to me.

KATRINE: It was you who pulled us out of good jobs in New York to come here. That was your last grand plan.

MARIAN: You had just as much reason to run.

KATRINE: I was following you, to back you up.

MARIAN: You were moldering, restoring old paintings.

KATRINE: Don't put the blame on me. You're the one who had to write, "*An Expose of the Gaming Industry from the Inside Out.*"

MARIAN: It's a damn good idea and I'm going to get it published.

KATRINE: That's one of your little contradictions. You want to run but you can't move. How many pages after two years?

MARIAN: You were packing the car at 5AM you were so goddamn eager.

KATRINE: Another version of your selective reality. I chained myself to the radiator. You sawed off my wrist.

MARIAN: You were stuffing the glove compartment with miniature vodka bottles.

KATRINE: You didn't think I was going to take the ride to hell sober, did you? Who do you think I am?

MARIAN: The Buddha.

KATRINE: Ha!

MARIAN: Who was it said, "If you meet the Buddha, kill him."

KATRINE: Lin Chi.

MARIAN: Showoff! I had to do all the driving.

KATRINE: If we're driving into the *wasteland*, yes, *you* have to drive.

MARIAN: You convinced me that since the Guggenheim and the Hermitage opened a branch at The Venetian the wasteland was blooming— Your art historian's dream.

KATRINE: I admit, the kinky marriage of casino and museum aroused me.

MARIAN: It's so you: the collision of high and low.

KATRINE: But the museums bailed—too bizarre. Almost as bizarre as us. Nope, *YOU'RE* why we're in Sin City. You thought if you could slip your PhD manacles you'd find a real man. You sure did.

MARIAN: You thought you'd snag yourself a rich gambler. But he turned into a rambler, didn't he?

PAUSE. SOMETHING SHIFTS IN KATRINE. SHE'S UNTETHERED...

KATRINE: Miguel didn't really leave.

MARIAN: Don't start—

KATRINE: He's going to send for me.

MARIAN: You promised me you'd stop!

KATRINE: You're a fine one to talk—you don't know what's real.

MARIAN: I know we survived a car crash.

KATRINE: See?! You're deluded!

MARIAN: You've denied it for seventeen years.

KATRINE: You make up more than I do!

MARIAN: I know the car door got ripped off and folded in two. I still see the bare steel gash where the red paint split along the fold. You concoct a fantasy: He's going to send for you. In what—his '39 Bentley? Why can't I see that? Could it be, it's not real?

PAUSE.

MARIAN: What? … What's wrong?

KATRINE: (drifting, disconcerted) Miguel was never here, was he?

MARIAN: Of course he was. Now you're going to the other extreme.

PAUSE. KATRINE SLOWLY LIFTS HER ARMS LIKE A HERON IN FLIGHT, AN ELOQUENT STUDY.

MARIAN: What are you doing?

KATRINE: I'm flying away from you.

MARIAN: What are you doing?!

KATRINE: I'm waving my arms. And wafting my legs. (pause) So where do *you* think he is?

MARIAN: You told me he passed his medic's training.

KATRINE: He sent me shots of himself in uniform in the desert.

MARIAN: Then you know where he is.

KATRINE: It could've been outside Vegas for all I know. Desert is desert.

MARIAN: And men are men.

KATRINE: You don't believe that.

MARIAN'S CONFLICTING IMPULSES JAM UP.

MARIAN: When Jess …

KATRINE FILLS WITH CONTRITION.

KATRINE: Our lives would be different if I never moved in.

MARIAN: We've been through all that—you weren't in your right mind.

KATRINE: It was my fault.

MARIAN: I thought I could save him.

KATRINE: Nothing could.

MARIAN: I'm not going to argue.

KATRINE: But you are.

MARIAN: Everyone can say no.

KATRINE: That's not true. Not everyone can say no.

MARIAN: Even you.

KATRINE: It's very hard for me; I'd rather say yes.

MARIAN: You make it sound like a virtue.

KATRINE: Just a reality.

MARIAN: There's no virtue in your reality?

KATRINE: Reality's fascinating, don't you find?

MARIAN: You've never figured it out.

KATRINE: That's the point.

MARIAN: You have a tendency to float off.

KATRINE: And you have a tendency to tie everything down.

MARIAN: There you go, playing the martyr again. Where is he? (no response) I can't see Miguel as a medic. If he saw someone's arm blown off, he'd puke. (no response) All right, I'm done.

KATRINE: So what's your plan?

MARIAN: First we quit our jobs.

KATRINE: Abandon the gambling biz! In Vegas?

MARIAN: The Baccarat table's seen the last of my sweet ass.

KATRINE: And what'll we do for money? Nobody here cares about the difference between a Monet and a Manet, only the money, and Blackjack's all I'm trained for. I'm not going to work at the Bunny Ranch.

MARIAN: Don't even talk about men.

KATRINE: The bank's trying to take my car; I can't quit. I told you I bribed the Repo Man two hundred bucks last week.

MARIAN: You were an angel before they showed up.

KATRINE: Are you saying *they* made me who I am?!

MARIAN: We were different. (pause) Where're you going?

KATRINE: Time to take the suckers' money.

MARIAN: We don't work tonight.

KATRINE: (ignoring her) Worst thing I've ever done.

MARIAN: That's why we need to walk away. From people addicted to losing.

KATRINE: They start with the fantasy that "tonight's the night that'll change my life." And they look so shattered when they leave.

MARIAN: Like the night Miguel decided to enlist.

KATRINE: It's not the same thing. You dared him. He didn't think it through.

MARIAN: How do you know?

KATRINE: I feel him breathe when I'm in the other room. I can read his mind.

MARIAN: You mean, you *could*.

KATRINE: What's the difference?

MARIAN: The tense.

KATRINE: Why didn't you come home last night?

MARIAN: Where were *you*?

KATRINE: Here.

MARIAN: Drunk.

KATRINE: My template for embracing daily life.

MARIAN: So you couldn't have known I wasn't here.

KATRINE: I slept in your bed.

MARIAN: You what!

KATRINE: I miss you. Where were you?

MARIAN: That's none of your business.

KATRINE: Aren't I my sister's keeper?

MARIAN: Why can't you stay out of my bed?

KATRINE: I was falling. Toppling over backwards in freefall. At first like a cannonball, then like a feather. I fell repeatedly against your pillow. All night. It's a wonder I don't have a concussion.

MARIAN: Falling's a bad habit.

KATRINE: And you're still wearing black—after a

year.

MARIAN: There are conventions.

LONG PAUSE.

KATRINE: I love you.

MARIAN: I know.

KATRINE: And what does convention suggest in this moment?

MARIAN: That I echo your sentiment.

KATRINE: Well?

MARIAN: Mother always would.

KATRINE: I'm waiting. (no response) How long are you going to punish me?

PAUSE.

MARIAN: I was with a man.

KATRINE: I see.

MARIAN: No, you don't.

KATRINE: You deserve it.

MARIAN: Nothing happened.

KATRINE: Is that what he'd say?

MARIAN: We just talked.

KATRINE: That's all anyone ever does.

MARIAN: No, sometimes they fuck. *You* might recall.

KATRINE: That's just talking.

MARIAN: Spoken by a woman who loves to talk.

KATRINE: Look who's talking.

MARIAN: We drove out to Red Rock Canyon.

KATRINE: Who was it?

MARIAN: Luke.

KATRINE: You took the barboy?

MARIAN: He's gay, and—

KATRINE: On the anniversary of Jess's death?!

MARIAN: My dear husband was never big on

dates.

KATRINE: You're crazy—he could tell time without a watch.

MARIAN: There was an awesome silence. The sunset made the canyon look like it was in flames. The wind shakes the reeds on the bottom so it looks like a river on fire.

KATRINE: That's beautiful, but I'm only interested in what happened next.

MARIAN: No. I slept in the back seat. He slept in the front.

KATRINE: You expect me to believe that?

MARIAN: I couldn't be *here*. I just couldn't face being in—

KATRINE: It's freezing in the desert at night. Where were you really?

MARIAN: And where is Miguel, really?

KATRINE: What is this? If you torture me long enough I'll finally confess something I DON'T KNOW?

MARIAN: DON'T TAKE THAT TONE! You're

hiding something from me and I won't stand for it.

KATRINE: You're suffocating me!

MARIAN: We can't live together any more. Are you going to leave or will I?

KATRINE: It's a little sudden to spring this on me, isn't it?

MARIAN: It's been a year ... hardly sudden.

LONG PAUSE.

KATRINE: I'll pack.

LONG PAUSE.

MARIAN: Where will you go?

KATRINE: I'll travel.

MARIAN: You don't have any money.

KATRINE: Do you think a woman who looks like this needs money?

MARIAN: I'm better looking than you and I need money.

KATRINE: Work it, girl.

MARIAN: Would you ever consider going back to Switzerland?

KATRINE: No, of course not! I hated the dresses they made us wear. The tutors telling us we were lucky to have such parents: "Diplomats are so calm." Hah!

MARIAN: You loved the meals. Chilean Sea Bass Meuniere. Lapin a la sauce Sancerre.

KATRINE: And you were such a nasty girl, always hiding food in your underwear for later.

MARIAN: Don't go.

KATRINE: I'll stay on one condition.

MARIAN: You're going to blackmail me?

KATRINE: Yes.

MARIAN: I won't stop talking about the accident.

KATRINE: Then I need to pack.

MARIAN: Then I have a condition of my own.

KATRINE: Perpetual negotiator. Yes?

MARIAN: If I bury the accident, you forget about Miguel.

KATRINE: I don't want to forget about—

MARIAN: When the car hit the tree Mother and Father—

KATRINE: There was no tree.

MARIAN: You had a concussion.

KATRINE: There was no tree.

MARIAN: You lost your memory for three weeks.

KATRINE: They left us. And you've refused to tell me where they went.

MARIAN: I took you to Arlington.

KATRINE: I don't know why. Because they're not dead.

MARIAN: You saw their graves.

KATRINE: Only soldiers get buried there.

MARIAN: And diplomats.

KATRINE: I can't forget Miguel.

MARIAN PRODUCES A LETTER.

MARIAN: This came today.

KATRINE: Bravo! A new tactic?

MARIAN: It's from the Army.

KATRINE DOUBLES OVER FROM WHAT SHE FEARS IS NEWS OF MIGUEL'S DEATH.

KATRINE: He's … not …

MARIAN: No. He's alive.

KATRINE: Then …

MARIAN: It's from Fort Stewart.

KATRINE: He's not—he left there after basic.

MARIAN: Still his home base. They've written to advise you that he's deserted, and you're warned to report any contact.

KATRINE: Give me that!

MARIAN: Under penalty of law. It's a federal offense, abetting a deserter.

KATRINE: Marian! You opened my mail!

LONG PAUSE. MARIAN HANDS KATRINE THE LETTER.

MARIAN: He's probably coming here.

KATRINE: (reading) He's been AWOL for almost six weeks.

MARIAN: The penalties include Federal prison.

KATRINE: We're not turning him in.

MARIAN: I wouldn't think of it.

KATRINE: I'm going to find him.

MARIAN: Why? First he deserts you, then he deserts the army.

KATRINE: He never would've gone if you didn't push him. Why'd you do it?

MARIAN: Because he was ranting we needed to teach *them* a lesson. I had to point out *he* was never going to do the *ass kicking*.

KATRINE: Well you underestimated him, didn't you? Just like you—

MARIAN: Katrine! This is Vegas. This isn't our formal garden in the Geneva Academy for Girls. This is the home of five-dollar wedding chapels, nuclear testing, legal prostitution, and Creationism. This is where they shoot abortion doctors but defend torture. How far do you think you're going to get?

KATRINE: May I take your suitcase?

MARIAN: You've got your own.

KATRINE: Yours is bigger.

MARIAN: Why do you always want what's mine?

KATRINE: 'Cause you always got more.

PAUSE.

MARIAN: (thaws) He's probably strutting down the Strip right now, slipping hundred dollar chips to broken old gamblers.

KATRINE: Your overheated imagination almost got you expelled.

MARIAN: It never stops.

KATRINE: It needs to sleep.

MARIAN: It's worse when I sleep.

PAUSE.

KATRINE: I like that you see him helping an old gambler.

MARIAN: I never said— I only said he was trouble.

KATRINE: But you never had a problem with trouble.

MARIAN: That's right. After I met Jess I decided I had to live with it. Better than not …

PAUSE.

KATRINE: I am sorry for your loss.

PAUSE.

MARIAN: Now I believe you.

KATRINE: That doesn't mean I see why you're still wearing that black dress! CHRIST! Marian!

MARIAN: What's wrong with you?

KATRINE: You don't want me to find Miguel.

Because you're angry Jess's gone, and you blame me. Admit it!

MARIAN: Control yourself, Katrine.

KATRINE: The matron isn't going to come in and cane you, Marian, if you raise your voice.

MARIAN: I can be emotional without bellowing drunkenly around the room.

KATRINE: Every moment we're living should be played like the third act. Get into it, baby.

MARIAN: Forgive me when I don't take what you say at face value. It must be your performance that throws me off.

KATRINE: Oh darling, we've got to get you into some red!

MARIAN: I'm not ready.

KATRINE: Well, then I'm going to look for Miguel.

MARIAN: Wait!

KATRINE: You'll get out of the black?

MARIAN: Yes.

KATRINE: Then I'll stay a little longer. (pause) Well?

MARIAN IS ALMOST OUT OF THE ROOM ON HER WAY TO CHANGE WHEN KATRINE STOPS HER.

KATRINE: Why did you read my mail?!

MARIAN: To protect you.

KATRINE: That's not in your power.

MARIAN: Is that what this is about? You think I want power?

KATRINE: Yeah!

MARIAN: I just want to be your sister.

KATRINE: That's fine—just do that!

MARIAN: How can I be if I don't try to save you?

KATRINE: From what?!

MARIAN: Yourself!

KATRINE: Who's still wearing black a *year* after her husband got— If I were trying to save you I'd rip that goddamn shroud off your body.

MARIAN: You know what I'll do if you get violent.

KATRINE: All right, I'll take you for a waltz through the maze of our garden—remember?

MARIAN: I'm the one who remembers.

KATRINE: The juniper sap used to stick to my fingers and harden like the amber that entombs prehistoric insects. (pause) That memory makes me want to peel the black right off you.

MARIAN: See how your mind goes all balooey there? I want it unvarnished, devoid of strategy, without nuance, no vibrato, blunt, crude, clear, straight tone.

KATRINE: You're asking too much.

MARIAN: Your cynicism breaks my heart.

KATRINE: Believing an ounce of illusion might be a necessary evil isn't cynical; it's healthy.

MARIAN: Just give it to me plain.

KATRINE: When you found me and Jess— The way you broke down and wailed. Anybody would scream, but you—

MARIAN: How dare you!

KATRINE: But you took it to the level of *Gothic horror*, and that's what finally broke him.

MARIAN: You don't have the right!

KATRINE: Of course, we're not supposed to talk about that!

MARIAN: (deliberately provoking KATRINE) Insensée, où suis-je? [Insane, where am I?]

KATRINE: Stop it! I hate French! I'll never go back there!

MARIAN: Où laissé-je égarer mes voeux?! [Where did I abandon my vow?]

KATRINE: You were always so perfect, but he was full of cracks!

MARIAN: And you found them all, didn't you?

KATRINE: Face it: Neither of us understands what happened.

MARIAN: I saw it with my own eyes.

KATRINE: It had nothing to do with sex.

MARIAN: Then what were you doing in the bathtub? Chatting?

KATRINE: Why has it taken you a year to ask me?

MARIAN: Tell me!

KATRINE PAUSES TO GATHER HERSELF.

KATRINE: I was in the bath, getting ready for work. He came in. I was startled.

MARIAN: Why didn't you tell him to get out?

KATRINE: It was like he didn't even see me. He sat down on the toilet and put his head in his hands and started sobbing. I said, Jess? Then he looked at me. I said, I'm in the bath, and then I thought, what a stupid thing to say, of course he can see that. (pause) His head dropped back in his hands. What's wrong? He said he'd lost everything gambling, the house, the car … He owed four hundred grand and had no way to get it. He didn't know how to tell you. (pause) The bath water got cooler. Then he looked at me. He wasn't leering. He was just looking real slow. He drank in my body like he was parched. And then my eyes. I held out my arms.

MARIAN: Oh … god … no …

KATRINE: Do you want me to stop?

MARIAN: … No …

KATRINE: He took off his clothes, and his tears stopped. When he got in the tub the water flooded.

MARIAN: That's enough.

LONG PAUSE.

MARIAN: Why didn't you tell me this?

KATRINE: You told me you didn't want to know.

MARIAN: I couldn't.

KATRINE: Why?

MARIAN: With him dead I only had you. And if I threw you out, then I'd be alone. And I couldn't.

KATRINE: Didn't you see the pain he was in?

MARIAN: Yes.

KATRINE: And why didn't you do anything?

MARIAN: All year I fought my instinct to hurt you, and now you want to pry open the cracks of yet another damaged man. Get rid of him.

KATRINE: Just throw him away?

MARIAN: Find someone who isn't damaged.

KATRINE: Have you looked at where we live?

MARIAN: That man could be the death of you.

KATRINE: And then you'd be all alone? (no response) So, your suitcase?

MARIAN: I certainly won't need it.

KATRINE: Stop thinking that way. You can get out of here.

MARIAN: What good is running from something inside us?

KATRINE: I don't get you.

MARIAN: Wherever we go, there it'll be.

KATRINE: What?

MARIAN: What you're running from.

KATRINE: And what is that?

LONG PAUSE.

MARIAN: You ran away from the consulate.
Then when Aunt Ginny and Uncle Crane brought
us back from Geneva we didn't exactly last long in
Greenwich.

KATRINE: It's your fault they sent us away. You
exaggerated about poor Uncle Crane.

MARIAN: How many times does a man have to
accidentally walk in on you in the bathroom before
you sense a pattern? Then we ran away from Miss
Porter's School.

KATRINE: So? We went back.

MARIAN: They made us. Sometimes you're so
illogical—we still ran. Being orphaned is
dangerous.

KATRINE: I'm not an orphan. And you didn't
have to tell Aunt Ginny. He never touched you.
You're the reason we're always running. How
many apartments is this? The landlords keep
kicking us out after you sledgehammer the
bathtub.

MARIAN: I have a problem with bathtubs. Why

is that?

KATRINE: Why was the receipt for the sledgehammer in my bed?

MARIAN: If you find him, you've walked right back into the problem.

KATRINE: So, if I know that, then I'm not running, am I?

MARIAN: Winning the debate isn't always the point, *Katrine*.

KATRINE: Who told you that, *Marian*?

MARIAN: Father.

KATRINE: When?

MARIAN: The day of the accident.

KATRINE: No.

MARIAN: It was morning and we were in the parlor. You were hurling yourself all over the divan. He was shouting at us for—

KATRINE: We never got in the car.

MARIAN: You started crying, "she started it," and

Father—

KATRINE: Okay! I've seen Miguel.

MARIAN: I knew it!

KATRINE: In my mind.

MARIAN: (with grudging admiration of KATRINE's parry) Smooth.

KATRINE: The security cameras capture two heart attacks at each end of my blackjack table. I open a suitcase and slam down dozens of card decks. Every one torn. I throw them away. In runs Miguel: Come with me! I freeze. Just then a bullhorn: Private Morales, come out with your hands on your head. I yank his arm: C'mon, I'll hide you behind the one-way mirror. Miguel moans: That's where you live. I snarl: It's why you left me. He protests: I didn't leave you, I enlisted. I can't stand it—I kiss him: Damn, I missed you. I shove him through the security door and hit a fire alarm. The crowd stampedes. I fill my suitcase with the torn decks.

MARIAN: That's a poem.

KATRINE: That's a chase scene.

MARIAN: Poems are chase scenes.

KATRINE: No, a poem is a way to plumb the depth of an experience by compressing it to the perfect words.

MARIAN: It's not perfect?

KATRINE: It's a suitcase of discarded objects.

MARIAN: Like you?

KATRINE: Like you?

MARIAN: I wasn't "discarded." I was left alive by a man who ... And what were you if not discarded?

PAUSE.

KATRINE: You can feel Miguel's coming back.

MARIAN: I can't feel any such thing.

KATRINE: Yes, you do, because you feel what I feel.

MARIAN: No I don't.

KATRINE: You told me so yourself many times, my *dear sister*.

MARIAN: Ah, so you haven't forgotten?

KATRINE: I can't forget we're sisters any more than I'm my mother's child. OUR mother, the hour-long mother, the mother of the hour!

MARIAN: Are you drunk?

KATRINE: Maybe.

MARIAN: Do you know what time it is?

KATRINE: I think it's 11:30. Am I right?

MARIAN: At night, yes.

KATRINE: Good, I was pretty sure it was night.

MARIAN: You're late for work if you're really supposed to go in.

KATRINE: I can't.

MARIAN: I see that.

KATRINE: Sowshit. You can't see anything but my perfect mask.

MARIAN: You're *transparent* to me, darling.

KATRINE: I *loathe* that kind of talk!

MARIAN: Don't get maudlin on me. I was playing with you.

PAUSE.

KATRINE: We used to play so well.

MARIAN: Yes …

KATRINE: Marian?

MARIAN: Hmmm …

KATRINE: Remember when we played Pyramus and Thisbe?

MARIAN: (laughing) No.

KATRINE: Obviously you do.

MARIAN: Remember when you pretended to be the wall's echo?

KATRINE: I love echoes. You were so funny when you'd answer.

MARIAN: We had such fun.

KATRINE: We did.

MARIAN: Hmmm …

KATRINE: Why can't we be like that again?

MARIAN: I don't know … why not?

KATRINE: Yeah … why not?

MARIAN: Come here.

KATRINE: What?

MARIAN: Hug me.

KATRINE: That's good.

MARIAN: Tighter.

KATRINE: That's as tight as I can.

MARIAN: You wuss, come on, squeeze.

KATRINE: No judgments.

MARIAN: Don't start.

KATRINE: No, wait, Marian, let's hold on to this for just a little longer.

MARIAN: Okay. (Long pause) I don't want anything but this feeling. Remember when we floated all day in the vice-consul's pool, soaking up that sun? We could still be there ...

KATRINE: But then Mother slapped the butler because he spilled a tray of canapés.

MARIAN: No, stay with the peace.

KATRINE: Certainly. Would you like to dance, my dear?

MARIAN: Yes, my darling, I would. Shall we?

THEY DANCE.

KATRINE: Remember that French Swiss kid who was in love with you?

MARIAN: You were jealous!

KATRINE: How could I be? Every time he tried to approach you he'd get a hard-on, and had to walk away before anyone noticed.

MARIAN: You were jealous because I inspired passion!

KATRINE: (laughing) It's true that you were a beauty.

MARIAN: Are.

KATRINE: Are.

MARIAN: Stay on the beat.

KATRINE: Marian...

MARIAN: Just dance.

THEY CONTINUE DANCING AS THEY TALK.
THEY DANCE WELL TOGETHER.

KATRINE: Why'd you fall in love with Jess?

MARIAN: When I first interviewed him outside
the Baccarat room I thought he was the most
elegant man I'd ever seen. He was aloof at first.
He was winning and he couldn't afford to break
his concentration; bets were ten thousand a hand.
He was on his way back to the table, but
something about my question caught him.

KATRINE: What was it?

MARIAN: "Do you ever gamble with love?"

KATRINE: Shameless.

MARIAN: I was writing a book—by any means
necessary! He ushered me to his seat at the table
and asked me to play his hand. We won fifteen

thousand. He gave it to me.

KATRINE: Shameless.

MARIAN: To fund my book! I hid from him for a week.

KATRINE: And from me.

MARIAN: He found my dissertation online, used his brilliant mathematical chops to hack the database, and filled my pages with feedback, more generous and erudite than my Columbia professors, and left it—with a single lily—outside my door. That did it.

KATRINE PULLS AWAY. PAUSE.

KATRINE: I don't know how to give him up.

MARIAN: You don't even have to! HE'S NOT HERE.

KATRINE: I love him.

MARIAN: How much longer can you teeter on the edge?

KATRINE: There goes your imagination again. You said you wanted it straight, right? Well here it is: You want control, but you're a living earthquake. My sister: QuakeWoman. *Watch her shake, rattle, and roll.* That's why you attract the dark ones. They feel the upheaval underneath, and that lures them in. They yearn for your cure, but that's a laugh because deep down they know they've swerved into the Red Zone. (no response) Isn't that right?

MARIAN: You have a fantasy of Miguel waiting in the desert, don't you?

KATRINE: I'm painting on the wall: "I—DON'T—KNOW—WHERE—HE—IS."

MARIAN: If you're lost in fantasy, how can I help you?

KATRINE: I don't need your help. I have my own path.

MARIAN: But it can't exclude me! If you decide on your *path* that you're going to drive off a cliff, then I need to *know*, or I'm the one who let her sister drive off a cliff, and that's why—

KATRINE: All right! I'll make sure you know!

MARIAN: How generous of you. Take a breath.

KATRINE: Take your own goddamn breath!

MARIAN: On the count of three.

KATRINE: You're the one who's insane, not me.

MARIAN: One.

KATRINE: Deranged.

MARIAN: Two.

KATRINE: All right.

MARIAN: Ready … three.

THEY BREATHE DEEPLY. LONG PAUSE.

KATRINE: I can hear our connection.

MARIAN: Breath can be loud.

KATRINE: No … deeper.

PAUSE.

MARIAN: Let's go to bed.

KATRINE: It's only midnight.

MARIAN: It's been a long day.

KATRINE: The day he died.

MARIAN: And now it's over. I think I could sleep.

KATRINE: Then go.

MARIAN: I can't sleep if I don't know you're safe at home.

KATRINE: I'm not the one driving into the desert.

MARIAN: It was the canyon.

KATRINE: It's in the desert.

MARIAN: He didn't touch me.

KATRINE: I don't care. I care about the desert. Why'd you go out there?

MARIAN: It's the opposite of those juniper-hedge labyrinths in Geneva. It's empty.

KATRINE: No it's not. It's full of scorpions.

MARIAN: I'm not afraid of them. I saw this group of scorpion hunters. Just little boys. I asked what they were doing. Pharmaceuticals. They were getting paid for every one they brought back alive.

KATRINE: Did you check your clothes?! The car?!

MARIAN: Most scorpions aren't venomous enough to kill us.

KATRINE: Who told you that?

MARIAN: Jess.

KATRINE: He's dead.

MARIAN: Sometimes … you can be so cruel.

KATRINE: I'm sorry. (no response) All right, I'll go to bed. (no response) It's past midnight. The year of ritual mourning is over.

MARIAN: (referring to Jess) How could you do it?

KATRINE: You wouldn't understand.

MARIAN: Of course I wouldn't.

KATRINE: There was a hunger in his eyes.

MARIAN: That was for me.

KATRINE: It was always there.

MARIAN: You said that was the only time.

KATRINE: It was … He died that night …

MARIAN: But?

KATRINE: It was only once, but it might have been forever. It was like lying in a bath of desire. I dissolved. I was lost.

MARIAN: You never get lost.

KATRINE: This was a different kind of lost. Completely liquid.

MARIAN: I don't understand.

KATRINE: Yes you do. (no response) Wake me before you go, will you?

MARIAN: All right.

KATRINE: Good night.

MARIAN: Good night.

KATRINE: I love you.

MARIAN: Go to bed.

ACT II, SCENE 1

4AM. MARIAN IS SITTING IN THE DARK, WAITING. KATRINE COMES IN FROM

OUTSIDE.

MARIAN: Where were you?

KATRINE: You scared me to death!

MARIAN: Are you drunk?

KATRINE: No.

MARIAN: You've seen him.

KATRINE: You look like a Caravaggio with the moonlight behind you.

MARIAN: In Rome or Naples?

KATRINE: I'd say it's—

MARIAN: Admit it! You went to see him!

KATRINE: No! I couldn't sleep, so I went to check on my car.

MARIAN: Don't lie to me.

KATRINE: Stop accusing me.

MARIAN: You locked that door like a whisper.

KATRINE: I didn't want to wake you.

MARIAN: I watched you get in the car with a bag—our food's gone.

KATRINE: ALL RIGHT!

LONG PAUSE.

MARIAN: You're going to help him?

KATRINE: Yes.

MARIAN: From *here*?

KATRINE: If we're running, we're both targets.

MARIAN: You're putting us at risk.

KATRINE: You're not involved.

MARIAN: Who's going to believe that?

KATRINE: We won't get caught.

MARIAN: Why not?

KATRINE: We're too careful.

MARIAN: So were Father and Mother.

KATRINE: I refuse to go there. I know where

every card is.

MARIAN: Gambling and life are different.

KATRINE: They're both games of chance.

MARIAN: If you didn't know I was watching you, then how will you fool the military police?

KATRINE: They aren't obsessed with catching me; they have lives.

MARIAN: I can't help you.

KATRINE: What does that mean?

MARIAN: I'm sorry.

KATRINE: You said that you wouldn't turn him in.

MARIAN: I changed my mind.

KATRINE: You can't do that!

MARIAN: You can't lie to me.

KATRINE: NO! He could get the death penalty!

MARIAN: Did he tell you that?! That man is such a— The army hasn't executed a man since '61.

KATRINE: You're lying!

MARIAN: I looked it up. He might do time, but he won't die.

KATRINE: You can't do this to me!

MARIAN: If I don't, you'll both go to prison. It's for your own good!

KATRINE: You've been waiting for this, haven't you? Doing your research, reading my mail, watching me in the night, you—

MARIAN: You've got to let him go!

KATRINE: NO!

MARIAN: You've got to!

KATRINE: NO! I WON'T!

MARIAN: I'm not giving you a choice!

LONG PAUSE.

KATRINE: Remember when we were little we'd play that game where we'd pretend I was you and you were me?

MARIAN: "Counterfeit."

KATRINE: We never played after the accident.

LONG PAUSE.

MARIAN: So you remember?

KATRINE: Yes …

MARIAN: Katrine …

KATRINE: I jumped up on the back seat to watch Daddy's hands on the steering wheel, and I saw this ice patch up ahead. It was gleaming in the sunlight and I thought it was beautiful. It was shaped like a dolphin, and I imagined that dolphins were jumping in front of us like they did in front of our boat in Monte Carlo. I felt safe with the dolphin guiding us, and I felt safe because Daddy was driving—I always felt safe in the car— and I said, "Follow the dolphin, Daddy." He said, "What, sweetheart?"

MARIAN: Why haven't you ever …

KATRINE: The car started spinning. I saw Mommy scream, but then my ears stopped. I tried to grab her, but the linen headrest on her seat came away in my hand, and I thought, I'm going to be in trouble. Out the windows the world was

going round and round like our carousel. It was
in slow motion, and it was so pretty I was
hypnotized. You grabbed my legs and tried to
pull me down, but I had to watch. I don't
remember anything after that.

MARIAN: Come here.

KATRINE: I don't know.

MARIAN: Come.

THEY EMBRACE.

KATRINE: That's it.

MARIAN: Don't let go.

PAUSE. KATRINE PULLS AWAY.

KATRINE: What are you going to do?

MARIAN: Nothing.

KATRINE: You promise?

MARIAN: Yes.

KATRINE: You'll help us?

MARIAN: Yes.

KATRINE: I'm cold.

MARIAN: I'll be right back.

KATRINE: Where are you going?

MARIAN: Getting a blanket.

KATRINE: Marian?

MARIAN: No, I don't want a drink.

KATRINE: Marian?

MARIAN: Here, wrap this tight.

KATRINE PUSHES MARIAN AWAY.

KATRINE: Don't touch me.

MARIAN: Don't turn this around. I'm not the bad one here. You're the one got us involved in a federal crime.

KATRINE: How can it be a crime to save the man I love?

MARIAN: If you love him, then why'd you say no when he proposed?

KATRINE: He wasn't ready.

MARIAN: Who wasn't? (no response) Where is he?

KATRINE: At the mouth of the Eldorado Canyon.

MARIAN: Good lord! What keeps him from burning up?

KATRINE: He found a ventilation shaft in the Techatticup Mine.

MARIAN: Outside Nelson?

KATRINE: Yeah.

MARIAN: That's a ghost town.

KATRINE: Not since Miguel arrived.

MARIAN: It's not safe. What about the tourists?

KATRINE: The army taught him how to disappear.

MARIAN: Oh … Katrine …

KATRINE: You sure you don't want a drink?

MARIAN: I don't need a glass.

KATRINE: I've never seen you drink from the bottle.

MARIAN: There's a lotta things you haven't seen.

KATRINE: He gave me a Rosy Two-tone Beardtongue.

MARIAN: Is that some sexual technique he learned over there?

KATRINE: No. (pause) It's a rare desert flower.

MARIAN: I thought you hated the desert.

KATRINE: That's before Miguel was in it. He took me to a clump of desertsmoke trees. We laid down. The blooms are purple and smell like smoldering musk.

MARIAN: How lovely for you.

KATRINE: This is why I didn't want to tell you.

MARIAN: Don't you think you should make a better plan than fucking him under a sweet smelling tree?!

KATRINE: Your jealousy is so obvious! Don't you think you should put yourself back together?

MARIAN: Am I getting any help from you?

KATRINE: He's a good man, and if you help him through this, then maybe you'd feel less like a corpse.

MARIAN: Your tongue ...

PAUSE.

KATRINE: Fine. Here's what we're going to do.

MARIAN: Mexico.

KATRINE: That obvious? Thousands cross the other way every day.

MARIAN: (almost a command) You're not going with him?

KATRINE: Just to get him across, then I'll be back.

MARIAN: Why am I always saying, I don't believe you?

KATRINE: Why don't you stop?

MARIAN: Why did you deny the accident all these years?!

KATRINE: I don't know ... how ... to say it ...

MARIAN: Try.

PAUSE.

KATRINE: Because if I stopped time, then I could wake up from a bad dream.

MARIAN: But look what you were doing. To me! Years of trying to convince you. Years of worry. How could you do that to me?!

KATRINE: If I let go, then I'd be the one who let them die. Why did you make me say this?

MARIAN: I'm fighting for the one person I've got left.

KATRINE: And what if you had to be alone?

MARIAN: We'll never be.

KATRINE: That's what Mother would always say. Night after night, sitting on our bedside. Aren't you just repeating what you were told?

MARIAN: Can you get him a fake passport?

KATRINE: I think so.

MARIAN: From who?

KATRINE: The beautiful Georgio.

MARIAN: I thought you were afraid of scorpions.

KATRINE: He's not so bad.

MARIAN: Don't con me. (pause) You didn't sleep with him?!

KATRINE: No!

MARIAN: Why would he do anything for you?

KATRINE: It's not me he'll do it for.

MARIAN: You expect *me* to ask him?

KATRINE: I've seen the way he looks at you.

MARIAN: This conversation is over.

KATRINE: Where are you going?!

MARIAN: None of your business.

KATRINE: It's four-thirty in the morning!

MARIAN: Is there anything you wouldn't do?

KATRINE: Don't go blundering around out there. You'll lead them right to him. They're watching us!

MARIAN: Already?!

KATRINE: Yes.

MARIAN: You know that?!

KATRINE: A car followed me home from work today.

MARIAN: What'd the driver look like?

PAUSE.

KATRINE: Do you remember the string quartet at the Grand Théâtre?

MARIAN: Was he in uniform?

KATRINE: Of course not. Do you remember the cellist?

MARIAN: Then how do you know?

KATRINE: When I went through a red light he followed me. I thought the sound of those strings must be the voices of angels singing.

MARIAN: Angels don't sing, they grunt.

PAUSE.

MARIAN: I'll talk to Georgio.

KATRINE: Oh Marian, thank—

MARIAN: Let me go.

PAUSE.

KATRINE: Angels do sing.

MARIAN: When?

ACT II, SCENE 2

*THE NEXT NIGHT. KATRINE IS WAITING,
PLAYING WITH A DECK OF CARDS. MARIAN
ENTERS.*

KATRINE: There's food in the fridge. (no response) Oh yeah, you're fasting. Was Georgio there? (no response) He can be such a shit. Ever since they made him a pit boss he thinks he's the Doge of Venice. (no response) Marian? (no response) Miguel told me the desert taught him patience. It's never been a virtue of mine, has it?

A LONG SILENCE. MARIAN IS QUIETLY

TRYING TO SING AS SHE DRINKS FROM THE VODKA BOTTLE

KATRINE: What did he say?

MARIAN: I've been thinking about the string quartet. When the cellist finished her last stroke and let her bow float to her side, the Grand Théâtre was filled with such a rich silence. We had earned the right to savor it. I thought, *please,* can we just sit here in this radiant silence? I hoped forever. But no, the first pair of hands struck, and the hall filled with thunder. Everyone rose. Mother's glance said, *rise,* and I rose. Always the good girl. Tears streaming down my face. I needed that silence to last … and it was gone.

KATRINE: I thought you were moved by the music.

MARIAN: I was …

KATRINE: But the tears weren't for the music.

MARIAN: No.

KATRINE: You were the last one to stop clapping.

MARIAN: It was the least I could do.

KATRINE: Father had to clamp your hands like a

vice.

LONG PAUSE.

KATRINE: What happened with Georgio?

MARIAN: We went to his office. He pressed me to the wall and unbuttoned my shirt. I said, can you get the passport? And he said, who for? I realized I'd never tell him—I can't trust him. I started to button my shirt. He grabbed my wrist, and I stomped on his foot.

KATRINE: Oh my god …

PAUSE.

MARIAN: I tried.

KATRINE: I'm so sorry.

MARIAN: No, I'm sorry.

KATRINE: No, no, I was wrong.

MARIAN: I couldn't.

KATRINE: I know. We don't need it.

MARIAN: If he knew Miguel's name, think what he could do.

KATRINE: Blackmail us.

MARIAN: He could report Miguel.

KATRINE: You're right—it can't work.

MARIAN: That son of a bitch.

KATRINE: That son of a ... Ahhh ... I'm such a ...

LONG PAUSE.

MARIAN: Are you driving out there tonight?

KATRINE: Yes.

MARIAN: Can I come? (no response) Oh ... (no response) You want to fuck your soldier in the desert, and I'd be in the way.

KATRINE: Marian, stop it, that's not it.

MARIAN: Or maybe you're afraid I'd tell him what I really think of him.

KATRINE: Oh, and what's that?

MARIAN: Never mind.

KATRINE: No, get your venom out!

MARIAN: Some things are private, even from you.

KATRINE: He says I can't get away from you soon enough; you're a leech!

MARIAN: If that sorry excuse for a man had been doing his job, then you wouldn't have ended up in the bath with my husband!

KATRINE: You're so primitive. You think if a man's banging away, then he's doing his JOB!

MARIAN: He's a deserter! In every way!

KATRINE: He didn't desert; he walked away from an illegal war.

MARIAN: *Ran* away.

KATRINE: He didn't desert me!

MARIAN: Then why'd you have a nervous breakdown when he shipped out?

KATRINE: Just to keep in practice.

MARIAN: Why'd I have to move you in with me and Jess?

KATRINE: Because you need to keep me close.

MARIAN: No. There wasn't room, not with—

KATRINE: Dig a little deeper. Do we choose men who're—how'd you put it?—"addicted to losing," so we can give 'em that last push?

MARIAN: People fail all on their own.

KATRINE: Take New York, for example.

MARIAN: No.

KATRINE: Saint Bernard, sweet Professor of Sociology, in—

MARIAN: Stop.

KATRINE: In love with you, wanted you to move in with him, and so you—

MARIAN: But he said you should find a new roommate.

KATRINE: Exactly. So you screwed another man.

MARIAN: It's my body—I can do what I want.

KATRINE: You sabotaged it, and when he confronted you, you mocked him, and he lost it and slapped you, and you hit him with a pan.

MARIAN: You weren't there!

KATRINE: Marian! I was in the next room! And it's a good thing because when I rushed in I found you trying to drown the groggy son of a bitch in the dishwater. If I wasn't there you'd be in prison now.

MARIAN: But you were there!

KATRINE: Always.

MARIAN: Jess was different.

KATRINE: A hero?

MARIAN: He worked. He built a business. Yes!

KATRINE: He was a boy.

MARIAN: Stop!

KATRINE: When I held his balls in my hand he shook like a leaf.

MARIAN: Stop it! Do you know how easily I could make a phone call?

KATRINE: I don't believe you could stoop that

low.

MARIAN: I didn't believe you could until I saw it.

KATRINE: You'll never forgive me, will you?

MARIAN: No.

PAUSE. KATRINE STARTS FOR THE DOOR.

MARIAN: What time will you be back?

KATRINE: Do what you have to do.

MARIAN: What time?

KATRINE LEAVES WITHOUT ANSWERING.

MARIAN: Katrine!

MARIAN OPENS HER CELL PHONE AND DIALS INFORMATION.

MARIAN: The number for the FBI, Las Vegas office …

ACT II, SCENE 3

DAWN. MARIAN IS ASLEEP ON THE FLOOR. KATRINE COMES HOME. SHE GENTLY STIRS MARIAN.

KATRINE: Darling ... I'm home ... (no response) Wake up ... Come on ... I need to talk to you ... (no response) You sleep like the dead, come on ... (MARIAN groans) That's it. Your loving sister's home ...

MARIAN: What time is ...

KATRINE: (pretending to celebrate) It's Mardi Gras!

MARIAN: What?

KATRINE: Fat Tuesday.

MARIAN: Where were— Are you calling me fat?

KATRINE: No. It's morning. What are you doing on the floor?

MARIAN: What are you ... on the floor?

KATRINE: You all right?

MARIAN: Tuesday?

KATRINE: It's not. I was teasing.

MARIAN: About what day it is?

KATRINE: Did you take some pills?

MARIAN: I don't know …

KATRINE: You need coffee.

MARIAN: I'm not fat!

KATRINE: Certainly not.

MARIAN: Where is he?

KATRINE: You're scaring me. Now wake up!

MARIAN: What are you doing?

KATRINE: I'm waking you up!

MARIAN: All right!!

LONG PAUSE AS MARIAN GAINS HER FOOTING.

KATRINE: I need to talk to you.

MARIAN: And I need to talk to you.

LONG PAUSE.

KATRINE: I don't know how.

MARIAN: Start anywhere.

LONG PAUSE.

KATRINE: I don't think I could live without you.

MARIAN: You may have to.

KATRINE: What does that mean?

MARIAN: What happened out there last night?

KATRINE: What happened here? What did you take?

MARIAN: People say goodbye forever each time they part. When you leave for work, when you go to the store, every time you walk out that door, you say goodbye forever.

KATRINE: No. Parting forever's an event.

MARIAN: It's in the eyes. Maybe 1/24th of a second, but it registers.

KATRINE: No.

MARIAN: When Jess left the night he died, I felt it.

KATRINE: No.

MARIAN: When you walked out last night.

KATRINE: No.

MARIAN: I felt it.

KATRINE: Then what am I doing here?

MARIAN: You want something, but you're gone.

KATRINE: You were way over the edge last night. I'm home. Do you want me to get down on my knees and beg?

MARIAN: I want you to pick up the pieces of that porcelain lamb you knocked off the mantle. I want you to—

KATRINE: That was when we were kids, are you—

MARIAN: I want you to drink all your cocoa without pouring it in the compote. Send the letter to Nana without wiping it—

KATRINE: Nana died years ago; you're scaring me.

MARIAN: You're breaking my heart.

KATRINE: I'm calling an ambulance.

MARIAN: For heartbreak? Ask Miguel about triage. A battlefield medic decides who to save and which ones to let go. Miguel's already gone. If we try to save him, we go down with him.

KATRINE: And you're never wrong!

MARIAN: No, I'm wrong more than ever. That makes it even harder.

KATRINE: To do what?

MARIAN: Do you know what'll happen to you in prison?

KATRINE: I'm in prison now. I can't find a new life because I can't afford one, and I can't go back because it's not there any more.

MARIAN: You have enough money to do anything you want.

KATRINE: You know I'm broke.

MARIAN: Then you're gambling.

KATRINE: I'm not.

MARIAN: Then what are you doing with your money?

KATRINE: This is why I said I'm in prison.

MARIAN: (realization dawning) You're giving it to him!

KATRINE: No!

MARIAN: Of course!

KATRINE: You're way off—

MARIAN: Now I get it! He was gambling, too, wasn't he?

KATRINE: Whatever you took last night has still got you.

MARIAN: Why else would he enlist? He was running. The same men who killed Jess want Miguel dead.

KATRINE: No! I don't admit to that.

MARIAN: Yes, and if you're with him they'll kill you, too, and you know it.

KATRINE: Enough! (pause) They're forcing me to pay his debt.

MARIAN: This is a real breakthrough.

KATRINE: I can never get away from you.

LONG PAUSE.

MARIAN: Last night when you left I called the FBI.

KATRINE: You WHAT?!

MARIAN: I called.

KATRINE: NO!

MARIAN: But when they answered, I almost vomited, and I threw the phone down.

KATRINE: That's it, I'm leaving!

MARIAN: No, *I'm* leaving! You drove me to the edge of betraying you. And I hate myself. Me! Betray you?! But you walked out on me, and I wanted to see you both in prison. Taking you back after Jess was the hardest thing I ever— but now I'm alone anyway.

MARIAN STARTS FOR THE DOOR.

KATRINE: He left me.

MARIAN IS ARRESTED.

MARIAN: When?

KATRINE: After we fell asleep last night, he must've gotten up. He wrote a note on the back of the shirt I brought him. When I woke up this morning he was gone. The shirt was over my steering wheel.

MARIAN: What are you going to do?

KATRINE: Work.

MARIAN: What about the debt?

KATRINE: I won't pay.

MARIAN: What will you do?

KATRINE: Just work.

MARIAN: There's something wrong with the way you're taking this.

KATRINE: Don't leave.

MARIAN: I have to.

KATRINE: No, you don't.

MARIAN: I thought we were sisters. I see now

that's an illusion.

KATRINE: It's a fact.

MARIAN: A biological accident.

KATRINE: No.

MARIAN: We couldn't be more separate.

KATRINE: No.

MARIAN: I have no idea who you are.

KATRINE: Nor do I. Do you think you know who you are?

MARIAN: You're such a child.

KATRINE: A child is someone who can't accept, but I can accept everything. At least I admit there are forces in me I don't understand. That makes me more of an adult than you— with your locked-up rules and your rigid illusions of boundaries, it's all a—

MARIAN: How can you possibly call me rigid? Because of you, Jess went out and deliberately provoked a loanshark until the bastard shot him. And I took you back!

KATRINE: I'm not asking for your forgiveness. I can stay without it. Maybe you'll find it. But I don't need it. I'm not your *little* sister any more.

MARIAN: You were leaving me!

KATRINE: Even if I went to Mexico I couldn't have *left* you. That's impossible.

MARIAN: I can rebuild my life without you.

KATRINE: We're each other's memory.

MARIAN: You pretended to have none.

KATRINE: I'm *with* you. That's everything.

MARIAN: You're not my memory.

KATRINE: Of course not— You remember the cellist lowering her bow, and I remember the tears in Mother's eyes when Daddy clamped your hands. But we heard the same music.

MARIAN: I don't hear music any more.

KATRINE: You're being so cruel. (pause) You actually called the FBI! How could you do that?

MARIAN: That's what I'm asking you.

KATRINE: All I did was try to help the man I love (or at least I thought I did). That doesn't hurt you—or us.

MARIAN: You smell death and you chase it.

KATRINE: I'm going to slap you if you keep insulting me like—

MARIAN: Then what were you *doing*?

KATRINE: Escaping from you. You drive people away from us.

MARIAN: No, don't you see? He played me. He didn't believe in the war.

KATRINE: He never said that.

MARIAN: Your deserter—slash—lover spent hours talking to me, waiting for you to come home.

KATRINE: You goaded him till he snapped.

MARIAN: No, think about it: He needed to get out, so he framed it as if I dared him to enlist. (no response) He already left you once. It ought to be easier the second time.

KATRINE: I think he was gone before he left me.

The war … Something was missing. He was staring at the desert, but he didn't see anything.

MARIAN: I hate that man.

KATRINE: I know you do.

MARIAN: I hate you.

KATRINE: And I hate you. Sometimes. And you know I don't.

MARIAN: You are the most infuriating person I've ever met.

KATRINE: Does that mean you'll forgive me?

MARIAN: No.

KATRINE: Then why couldn't you go through with the phone call?

MARIAN: Maybe if I leave I'll figure that out.

KATRINE: Not if you leave.

MARIAN: Why couldn't I stop clapping?

PAUSE.

KATRINE: What do I do with this grief?

MARIAN: I'm putting my suitcase next to the door.

KATRINE: Why?

MARIAN: I can't stay.

KATRINE: I know that feeling.

MARIAN: You'll help me pack?

LONG PAUSE.

KATRINE: Yes.

MARIAN: Yes?

KATRINE: Yes. (pause) Come here.

KATRINE ENFOLDS MARIAN IN HER ARMS.

THE END

Biographies

Matthew Maguire is a co-artistic director of Creation Production Company, which he founded with Susan Mosakowski. The company has produced forty-nine original works. His plays include *The Seven Deadly Elements*, based on the collage novel by Max Ernst, *The Memory Theatre of Giulio Camillo*, *The Tower*, and its solo version, *Babel Stories*, a science fiction opera, *Chaos*, with Michael Gordon, *Phaedra, Throwin' Bones*, which began as a collaboration with architects Elizabeth Diller and Ricardo Scofidio titled *Skin* at the Palais des Beaux Arts in Brussels, *Luscious Music*, which he performed as a solo at the Architecture Museum of Basel, and the OBIE Award winning *Abandon*, with a score by Andrew Ingkavet. His work also includes the creation with Philip Glass and Molissa Fenley of *A Descent into the Maelström* for Australia's Adelaide Festival. He is an active alumnus of New Dramatists, and served as chairman of the Theatre panel of the New York State Council on the Arts. His awards include fellowships from the NEA, the McKnight and Hammerstein Foundations, and commissions from the NEA, NYSCA, Meet the Composer, and the New York Foundation for the Arts. He received his MFA from NYU's Musical Theatre Writing Program. His writing has been published by Sun & Moon Press, Backstage Books/Watson Guptill, Manchester University Press, *TheatreForum, Performing Arts Journal,* and *The Drama Review*. He won an OBIE award for Performance in 1998 and an OBIE Award for Direction in 2007. He is the Director of the Theatre Program at Fordham College at Lincoln Center. For texts, collages, and other information go to:
www.creationproduction.org

Naomi Wallace's work has been produced in the United Kingdom, Europe, and the United States. Her work has received the Susan Smith Blackburn Prize, the Kesselring Prize, the Fellowship of Southern Writers Drama Award, and an Obie. She is also a recipient of the MacArthur "Genius" Fellowship. Her plays include *One Flea Spare, In the Heart of America, Slaughter City, The Inland Sea, The Trestle at Pope Lick Creek, Things of Dry Hours,* and *The Hard Weather Boating Party.* Her films include the award-winning, *Lawn Dogs,* available on DVD, and the 2009, *The War Boys,* co-written with Bruce McLeod.

NoPassport

NoPassport is a Pan-American theatre alliance & press devoted to live, virtual and print action, advocacy and change toward the fostering of cross-cultural diversity in the arts with an emphasis on the embrace of the hemispheric spirit in US Latina/o and Latin-American theatre-making.

NoPassport Press' Dreaming the Americas Series and Theatre & Performance PlayTexts Series promotes new writing for the stage, texts on theory and practice and theatrical translations.

Series Editors:
Jorge Huerta, Otis Ramsey Zoe, Caridad Svich

Advisory Board:
Daniel Banks, Amparo Garcia-Crow, Maria M. Delgado, Randy Gener, Elana Greenfield, Christina Marin, Antonio Ocampo Guzman, Sarah Cameron Sunde, Saviana Stanescu, Tamara Underiner, Patricia Ybarra